D0251401

MURPHY'S TRAIL

Also by Gary Paulsen

MURPHY'S TRAIL

Gary Paulsen
and
Brian Burks

Walker and Company
New York

First published in the United States of America in 1996 by Walker
Publishing Company, Inc.

Published simultaneously in Canada by Thomas Allen & Son Canada,
Limited, Markham, Ontario

Library of Congress Cataloging-in-Publication Data

Paulsen, Gary.
Murphy's trail/Gary Paulsen and Brian Burks.
p. cm.
ISBN 0-8027-4154-1
1. Murphy, Al (Fictitious character)—Fiction.   2. Sheriffs—West
(U.S.)—Fiction.   I. Burks, Brian.   II. Title.
PS3566.A834M89   1996
813'.54—dc20   96-13698
CIP

Printed in the United States of America

2   4   6   8   10   9   7   5   3   1

MURPHY'S TRAIL

CHAPTER 1

THE HEAVILY MUSCLED, line-backed dun stopped of his own accord on top of a gently sloped, mesquite-covered sandy ridge as if he knew his rider would want to take the time to survey the green ribbon of a valley below.

Al Murphy dropped the reins and swung stiffly to the ground. He stretched his aching legs, then took the once white, now dirt-brown bandanna from his neck, shoved his hat back, and wiped his brow.

The trail from Turrett, New Mexico Territory, to San Patricio, Arizona Territory, had been a long one. Murphy was glad the hurried trip was nearly over. By dark he'd be in the valley below, be in San Patricio, at last ending sixteen long days in the saddle.

Murphy took a frayed paper from his shirt pocket, carefully unfolded it, and read the sparse words.

> Señor Murphy,
> I need your help. There is no one else to turn to. Please come quickly.
>
> Risa

He gazed blankly at the horizon, his thoughts on the last and only time he'd been to San Patricio. Was it ten years ago, fifteen . . . a hundred?

His duties as a civilian scout for the U.S. Army were over. Victorio was dead, chased into Mexico and killed by the Mexicans, and Murphy had been headed nowhere in particular when he stopped in San Patricio for a few supplies and a bottle of whiskey. It was the bottle that had gotten him into trouble that day. Until recently, that same desire had all but destroyed him.

Five men, not counting the bartender, had been in the small adobe cantina that night. Rough-looking men, drunk and heavily armed. Three of them were playing cards at a table. Two stood at the bar, a makeshift affair made of boards resting on barrels.

The moment Murphy saw them, he knew they were long-riders, men who made their living taking whatever they wanted from whoever had it.

Murphy set his saddlebags on the floor beside one of the barrels. In them were ninety dollars, a pair of army-issue binoculars, two boxes of shells, and some stale hardtack: everything he owned outside of his horse, a saddle, his rifle, the clothes on his back, and an army-issue Colt .45 tucked in the waistband of his beltless khaki trousers.

The short, round Mexican bartender moved to him.

"Whiskey," Murphy said softly. "A bottle, no glass."

The two men at the bar were staring at him and he could feel the eyes of the three at the table on his back. He ignored them, tried to dismiss the mounting tension in the room. All he wanted was a bottle and he'd leave.

The bartender returned and Murphy reached in his pocket, hoping he had enough change to cover his purchase. If he had to reach in his saddlebags for money, the long-riders' interest in him would grow.

He looked in his hand. A quarter, two nickels, and four pennies. It wasn't enough. The cheapest rotgut he'd bought in years was four bits.

Anger flooded through Murphy. Reason told him to hand the change to the bartender and take whatever it would buy, but pride caused him to pick up his saddlebags, reach inside, and slam a shiny twenty-dollar double-eagle on the bar. He'd buy a case of whiskey if he wanted it and nobody was going to stop him.

The bartender took the eagle and went for change. Chairs grated on the floor behind Murphy, and the two at the bar slowly edged toward him. Murphy's anger changed to reckless rage. He knew these men weren't going to let him leave, knew that talking to them would be a waste of time.

He whirled, pulling the Colt. Guns boomed, seemingly from everywhere, making a continuous deafening roar. Murphy cocked his revolver and pulled the trigger without aiming, without knowing in the blur of action if his shot had any effect.

A bullet to Murphy's head ended his memory of the shoot-out; nearly ended his life. Days later he awoke. Risa Villabisencio was wiping his forehead with a damp towel. When he opened his eyes, she ran to the bedroom door, calling for her husband, Santiago. "Come quickly. The gringo is awake. I think maybe he will live."

For the better part of two months, Murphy stayed at the home of Santiago, Risa, and their two small sons, Antonio and Froylan. It was Santiago, a young lawyer and the un-designated leader of the small Mexican community, who'd, upon notification of the gunfight, had Murphy carried to his house. And it was Risa who had stopped the profuse bleeding from the deep bullet furrow in the back of his skull, staying up with him night after night while he was delirious with fever.

The dun stomped his foot to shake off a fly. Murphy glanced at him, then looked to the valley below. The years since the five long-riders had taken his saddlebags and left him for dead had changed Murphy. Then he was a good tracker, a fair shot with a rifle, but he'd had little experience with a handgun. Now he made his living with the Smith & Wesson double-action .44 on his hip.

He was sheriff of Turrett, New Mexico. Before that he had been the sheriff of Cincherville, and he'd been in so many fistfights, knife scrapes, and gun battles it was difficult for him to remember them all.

Scars covered his body as if his skin had been made by a patchwork-quilt seamstress. His bones ached when it was cold, and although he was only in his midthirties, he walked and looked like a much older man.

As Murphy pocketed the note his fingers brushed against the edge of his law badge. He unpinned it, wondering why he hadn't thought to remove it before now. His official jurisdiction had ended some six hundred miles to the east. He had no more authority here in Arizona than anybody else.

The dun shook his head and scratched the side of his sweaty headstall against his left front knee. Murphy slipped the badge into his saddlebags, grabbed the reins, and mounted. As the dun stepped out, Murphy puzzled over Risa's note.

It was a miracle her letter had reached him. The envelope, opened and resealed, had been addressed to the sheriff of Cincherville. How could Risa have known he had once lived there? He'd had no contact with her since the day he had left San Patricio years ago. What kind of trouble could she possibly be in, and why was it that no one else could help her?

Doesn't matter, Murphy told himself. Whatever the difficulty was, he'd do all he could, no matter how long it took. His duties in Turrett were just going to have to wait. He owed the Villabisencios—owed them his life.

CHAPTER 2

A LITTLE DUSKY light remained when Murphy entered the narrow main street of San Patricio. Other than a new, wider bridge across the creek, a few more houses, and the towering growth of dozens of cottonwoods scattered about, time had done little to change the village.

The reddish-brown mud walls of Pena's General Store still matched the color of the dust in the street, as did the front of the small livery and blacksmith shop across from it

Some laughing kids ran across the road, dragging a bunch of rattling tin cans tied to a string. The dun snorted and shied sideways. He would have bucked, Murphy believed, if he hadn't been so worn out.

Down the street on the right was the small, windowless cantina where Murphy had almost died. Murphy gently pulled the reins to slow the dun's walk as they passed by. Except for a bench outside for customers to sit on, instead of a log, the cantina hadn't changed either. The broken white plaster still appeared to be barely clinging to the walls.

One old mule was tied to the hitch rail and the door was open. Murphy fought the urge to stop. He wanted to wash the grime off his face, and a cool beer would soothe his dry throat and help him relax. But no, he had traveled too long too fast to waste time now. Unless they had moved, the Villabisencio hacienda was just ahead, hidden from view by the large Catholic church beside it.

Murphy marveled at the impressive, thick-walled two-story church building, just as he had done the first time he had seen it. Here was a poor town, a place barely alive,

5

where even a window was a luxury few could afford. Yet these hardworking Mexican peasants who fought the ground and the weather to provide the very minimum of necessities for their families obviously thought more of their God than they did of themselves.

The church had many windows, some of them stained glass, and the grounds were carefully manicured. Unlike the cantina, the church's thick plastered walls were in good repair and the entire structure had recently been white-washed.

Murphy turned up the rutted lane leading to the Villabisencios' U-shaped adobe home. He passed a small field of maize and stopped the dun in front of the courtyard, where a neatly rowed garden had been planted. A woman with a hoe in her hands, wearing a dark blue dress, stood near the center watching him.

"Risa?" Murphy called, not at all sure in the fast-fading light if this was the woman he knew.

She removed the scarf covering her head, wiped her face with it, and stepped toward him. It wasn't until she halted a few feet away, staring at him with dark, direct eyes and a grave face, that Murphy was positive. The years had stooped Risa's shoulders slightly, but her tapered face still bore a faultless complexion, high cheekbones, and a soft, wide mouth that perfectly complemented her nose and chin.

Her voice was strong, unintimidated. "Do I know you?"

Murphy swung from the saddle and ran a hand across his scruffy beard, remembering that he hadn't shaved since leaving Turrett. "You ought to. You looked at my ugly mug enough while doctoring the bullet hole in the back of my head."

Risa beamed with excitement as she stepped closer to him. "Is it you, Al? Is it really you?"

"It's good to see you again, Risa." Murphy dropped the reins and hugged her. She began to sob and her body trembled. After a long moment, Murphy pushed her back.

"I probably don't smell none too good. Haven't had a chance to take a bath in a while. Where's Santiago and the kids? Guess they aren't kids anymore."

Risa cupped her face in her hands, and it was a while before she regained her composure enough to speak. "I prayed. I knew you would come."

She touched his arm. "You look very tired. I will fix you something to eat. The old barn has fallen down, but behind the house is a corral. You can put your horse there."

Murphy led the dun, puzzled at her reaction when he had mentioned Santiago. Something must have happened to him, but where were their two sons, Froylan and Antonio? Perhaps they had married and now had homes of their own. No, they wouldn't be old enough for that, would they?

The new barn was nothing more than a crudely built pole lean-to with a large sheep pen behind, a pigpen on one side, and an empty three-stringer corral on the other. The corral wasn't much, barely substantial enough to hold a gentle horse, let alone a cow or a calf, yet it would do.

After unsaddling, watering, and feeding the dun, Murphy went to the back of the house and knocked loudly on the door.

Risa opened it. "You do not need to knock. This house is your house."

She turned and Murphy followed her into the kitchen. The room looked as he remembered it. A long wooden table with two high-backed chairs at the ends, an iron cookstove in the corner, and a metal washtub located under the only window in the room.

A bottle of tequila was set on the table beside a steaming hot cup of coffee. Murphy pulled the cork, took a long drink that burned down to his stomach, then poured a shot of the liquor into the coffee.

Risa was busy at the stove, obviously not ready to talk, so Murphy removed his hat, rolled up his sleeves, and went to the tub to wash. When he was through and seated, she placed a bowl of menudo and a stack of fresh tortillas in front of him.

"Sure looks good, Risa. Reminds me of what I've been missing all these years. Have you eaten?"

"Yes. I ate earlier." She poured herself a cup of coffee and sat down across from him. He swallowed a mouthful of the soup and glanced at her. Outside, he hadn't seen the streaks of gray in her long braids, hadn't noticed the dark rings around her eyes.

"What's happened, Risa? Why did you send for me?"

She nervously ran a finger around the rim of her cup. "You . . . you remember how everyone here would come to my husband for help? Whatever they needed, he would advise them what to do.

"When the gringo cattleman to the north stopped the water in the creek, it was my husband who went to the legislature and brought back a United States marshal to make him release the water.

"When the same man tore down the fences the small farmers here had built to protect their fields from the cattle, it was my husband who went to the court to plead for help from the law. When the cowboys came here to drink and they shot up the village and they violated a young girl, it was Santiago who went to the law in Tucson. The law would not do anything, so my husband went to see the governor. He made the law come here and arrest those men."

Risa raised her cup, blew gently on the coffee, and took a sip. "A year ago or more, a new cattleman, a tejano called Ben King, moved onto the mesa west of the valley. At first he left the village alone because he was too busy fighting the other gringos around him for more of the land. He has many men and he takes whatever he wants.

"A few months ago two Mexican goat herders and all of their goats were killed a short way from here, in the foothills below the mesa. Santiago, Antonio, and Froylan went there. King did not even try to cover up his horse's tracks.

My husband was able to follow them easily to King's rancho.

"You remember Santiago. He is a gentle, kind man who does not fight with fists or with a gun. But he is not afraid of anything. He met with King and told him he knew that he had murdered the two goat herders. Ben King laughed at my husband, shot bullets at his feet, and ordered him off the rancho. The next day Santiago took Antonio and Froylan with him to go to Tucson to get a . . . a . . ."

"Warrant?" Murphy interjected.

"Yes, that is it, a warrant. He found out that the United States marshal was away at Vera Cruz, so he left for there."

Her coffee cup shook as she again raised it to her lips, lowered it, and looked directly at Murphy. A cold wrath was in her as she continued. "My husband and sons did not reach Vera Cruz. A few of the men here went looking for them. They found our buggy. There was blood on the seats. The horses were gone. They tried to follow the tracks, but days had passed and a herd of cattle had been pushed over the trail."

Risa sighed. "Later, el señor Pena—you remember him don't you? He owns the store."

"Yes, barely. I think I only saw him a time or two."

"He and I went there to see for ourselves. The buggy was there, but we could not find anything else. We went to the marshal, who had returned to Tucson, and told him what had happened. We told him Ben King and his men had taken my husband and my sons and perhaps had already murdered them.

"He said he would look into it, but I know he will not. He is glad Santiago is gone. Now there is no one in San Patricio to bother him or to fight for the peasants' rights in the courts. Now King and the other gringos can do whatever they want to us."

Murphy picked up one of the tortillas, tore it in half,

and dipped it in the menudo. He believed Risa was right. Ben King had the motive. If no warrant was issued, there would be no arrest, and murder was a hanging offense. Still, Murphy wanted more information.

"How can you be sure it was King who took Santiago and the boys? Might have been a bunch of long-riders just looking for something to do or a vigilante group who spend their free time hating Mexicans."

"King took them," she snapped. "I know he did."

Murphy knew he needed more. Risa saying King had committed the crime was one thing, and proving it was another.

"Did anyone else follow King's tracks after finding the bodies of the two goat herders?"

"No. A boy had found the dead men and he came back to the village to tell. Many here were angry about the news, but my husband persuaded them not to go out there with him. He was afraid there might be more bloodshed."

Not enough, Murphy thought without speaking. Nothing she had said was enough to do anything legally. He started to tell her that, then changed his mind. It might start an argument and would serve no purpose.

His thoughts shifted. "How did you know I had been the sheriff of Cincherville?"

"Santiago told me. He found out from a man who came through here on his way to California. I do not remember what his name was."

Murphy wondered who it could have been, then shrugged, deciding it didn't matter. Information had a way of traveling across the west, sometimes with amazing speed.

Risa rose and went to the stove, returning with the coffeepot. She filled Murphy's cup and sat back down. "You said you had been the sheriff of Cincherville. Does that mean you are not there any longer?"

"No, I haven't been in Cincherville for a few years. I'm

sheriff of Turrett, New Mexico, now. It's a wonder I got your letter."

"It is because I prayed. I knew you would come if you could. No one has done anything here. No one will do anything. The courts, the government, the law, everything here is controlled by anglos. They don't care what happens to a Mexican. My husband knew this. That is why he spent his life fighting them."

A thin smile formed on Murphy's lips. "I'm an anglo and he didn't fight me. He and you worked real hard to save my life."

"Yes, but that is different. You were in need of help. Santiago is a kind man. He will help anyone."

Murphy pushed the empty bowl away, scooted his chair back, and took the makings from his shirt pocket. Risa watched quietly until he had the cigarette built and lit before speaking.

"It is because you are a sheriff and because you are white that the law will listen to you. You will help me, won't you?"

"Of course I will. I'll do everything I can." Murphy put the cigarette to his lips and inhaled deeply. "Are you sure there isn't anything else you can tell me?"

Risa shook her head. "No, I have told you everything." She paused a long moment, looking down. "I know my husband is probably dead. But perhaps my sons live. They have never harmed anyone."

Murphy doubted it. Too much time had passed and the chance that Santiago or the boys were alive was almost non-existent, especially considering the blood that had been found on the buggy seats.

"How old are your sons now?" he asked.

"Froylan is eighteen and Antonio is sixteen."

Murphy took another puff on the cigarette. Suddenly he was tired, very tired; the food mixed with the alcohol had dulled his senses, making him sleepy.

He stood. "I'll be leaving in the morning. Is there some-one here who could lend me a fresh horse?"

"Yes. El señor Pena has a horse, a good, big horse. I think he will lend him to me. Where are you going?"

"Like everyone else, guess I'll have to start with the buggy, if it's still there."

CHAPTER 3

THE SUN WAS high in the east when Murphy rode out of San Patricio on the trail leading to Tucson. Beneath him, the aged sorrel Risa had borrowed pranced as if he were a young colt. Al didn't like the large horse, didn't like his rounded withers, his rough gait, or the high way he held his head, but the dun needed a rest and for now the sorrel would have to do.

Murphy pulled his gray, sweat-stained Stetson to the side to better shade his deeply tanned face. He felt good. Before going to bed at Risa's, he had taken a bath and shaved. This morning he awoke to find Risa had washed the two sets of clothes he had brought with him, hanging them above the stove to dry overnight.

After a heaping breakfast of ham and eggs, Risa helped him put together a crude map showing where San Patricio was in relationship to Tucson and Vera Cruz, where the King ranch was located, and the approximate area outside of Vera Cruz where the buggy was found.

Tucson was some sixty miles to the north, and Murphy decided to make it his first stop before going on to the buggy. If the marshal was in, he wanted to talk to him. It was possible that Risa's judgment of what the law was doing was incorrect. More than once an angry widow had accused Murphy of doing nothing to find and arrest a killer when in fact he was doing everything he could.

The miles went by slowly and Murphy's thoughts drifted to Santiago and the boys, to one of the last times he had been with them. It was a Sunday, he remembered, because

Risa was angry with them for not going to church with her. Instead, they went fishing in the creek.

As always, no matter what he was doing or where he was going, Santiago wore a black coat, white shirt, and bolo tie. His mustache and long sideburns were perfectly trimmed on a young-looking, almost boyish face. Antonio and Froylan, who both looked more like their mother, were young then, barely big enough to carry the bucket of earth and worms between them.

They were happy kids who enjoyed playing tricks. A smile formed on Murphy's face as he remembered trying to put his foot inside a boot containing a small, writhing garden snake. Another time it was a frog, and why so many crickets had wanted to make his boots their home was always a mystery to him. To this day, he still shook and dumped his boots before putting them on.

Santiago wasn't above a little mischief either. While they were at the creek and their lines were in the water, Murphy lay down on a grassy spot and fell asleep. Heavy tugs on his cottonwood branch pole woke him and he scrambled to his feet, shouting.

"I got one. I got a big one."

The fish turned out to be the end of Santiago's line, which had been purposely tied to Murphy's. Santiago kept a straight face while explaining that he was sure a very smart turtle named El Farsante was responsible. The boys laughed until their sides hurt, then spent the rest of the day reminding Murphy about his big fish.

Yet there was a serious side to Santiago, a side that at times consumed him. For days the small, thin man would stay in his study, reading and taking notes from stacks of thick law books. He had been educated in Mexico, had mastered the English language perfectly, and had elected to spend his time and energy on the legal needs of the poor and oppressed in the area.

How he made enough money to live on, Murphy never

knew, but now and then one of the peasants would bring by a crate of chickens, a goat or hog, or a basket of produce.

Murphy's thoughts brought him back to the present. It wasn't right that wicked men prospered while honest men like Santiago hardly got by. And now he and his two sons were more than likely dead, murdered by bloodthirsty cutthroats who continued to gain all the riches this world had to offer.

Murphy reached in his saddlebags for one of Santiago's cigars. Risa had put several of them there before he left that morning. He looked at the cigar and became more resolved than ever. No matter how long it took, no matter where the trail led him, he'd bring Santiago's killers to justice or take his last breath trying.

The streets of Tucson were busy, considering the late hour. Murphy guessed the time to be close to midnight. He'd been here years ago, while working for the army, but then the town was just a village, much like San Patricio, with a population of three or four hundred at best. Now Tucson appeared to house ten times that number.

Probably the new mines in the area were causing the boom, Murphy guessed, and the arrival of the railroad, which allowed exports of livestock, wool, and other agricultural products while at the same time bringing in much needed mine, farm, and irrigation machinery.

Arizona was growing fast. Almost every newspaper Murphy had seen in the last year had at least one article about the rich strikes around Prescott, Tucson, and Tombstone. If the high-grade ore continued to hold, there would be no limit to the expansion the territory would see in the next few years.

Singing accompanied by a banjo and piano was coming from inside a saloon. Murphy reined into the only empty spot at the hitch rail and dismounted. He was tired, thirsty, sore, and his feelings toward the sorrel had changed from dislike to intense hatred. The horse's abnormally rough gait had done nothing but torture him into appreciating a *good* horse when he rode one.

Two drunks doing a poor job of holding each other up staggered out of the saloon. Murphy stepped through the bat-wing doors into a crowded room reeking of cigar smoke and whiskey. He made his way to the bar, and presently one of two bartenders waited on him.

"What'll it be?"

"A beer, cold if you've got it, and a shot of whiskey on the side." The bartender turned and Murphy stopped him. "Would you know if the U.S. marshal's in town?"

"He's here all right." The ruddy-faced man pointed past Murphy. "That's Dodson standin' over there by the roulette wheel. He's been there all day."

"Is he winning?"

The man shook his head with a blank look and walked away.

When his drinks came, Murphy paid for them, drank the shot of whiskey in one swallow, and took his beer with him as he made his way through the crowd to the roulette game. The information from the bartender bothered Murphy. Why would a lawman spend all day and half the night in a saloon? Didn't he have anything else to do? And what lawman made enough money to be able to gamble this long on a losing streak?

The operator spun the wheel while Murphy quietly observed the drunken, fair-haired man who wore a star on the lapel of his ruffled brown coat. A two-day stubble of beard couldn't hide the paleness of the marshal's cheeks which hinted that he was either in poor health or spent most of his time indoors. The marshal took a drink from the bottle in his hand and nervously watched the wheel stop.

"Six-black," the operator said loudly. "Two winners, one loser."

The marshal was unmistakably the loser. His face was tight and he was searching his wallet for more money. Murphy knew his timing wasn't the best, but he needed to talk to the man and there was no point in waiting.

"Marshal Dodson?" he said, stepping closer.

The lawman offered no greeting, just stared with challenging, bloodshot eyes.

"Name's Murphy and I was hoping you could help me. I'm looking for a fellow. Santiago Villabisencio. Thought you might know where I could find him."

"Never heard of him," the marshal mumbled, putting two bills on the board.

Murphy's temper flared. He wanted to tell the man he was a liar, that Santiago's widow had reported her husband missing months ago, yet he held his tongue. He'd learned over the years to never show his hand any more than he had to when investigating a case. The object was always to gain information, not give it.

"Are you sure? Word has it that he's been around these parts a long time."

"Look," Dodson's jaws tightened. "As you can see, I'm a little busy here and it's not my job to remember every greaser in the territory. If you've got a crime to report, do it, or get on with your business."

Murphy's anger was pushing him; it was all he could do to keep from landing his already clenched fist squarely on Dodson's chin.

"Thanks for your valuable time, Marshal," Murphy said contemptuously, then wheeled and headed back to the bar.

Risa was right, he thought, setting his glass down. The law wasn't going to be any help. What infuriated Murphy even more was that the honest, hardworking, and underpaid lawmen didn't need men like Dodson tarnishing their profession and creating public distrust that caused their job to be more difficult than it already was.

The bartender approached. "Ready for another one?"

Murphy gulped down the last of his beer and shook his head. He wanted another drink, wanted several more drinks, but he had learned to be careful. Alcohol had once controlled him, nearly killed him, and he drank it now only with temperance and respect.

Outside, he leaned against a veranda post and rolled a cigarette. He was puzzled. Risa had talked like Santiago was well known to the courts and lawmen in the area. So well known that the marshal may have considered him somewhat of a pest and was glad that he was out of the way. Why then would Dodson deny knowing Santiago? What purpose could his memory loss serve?

Probably nothing, Murphy thought, striking a match on the post and lighting his smoke. Dodson was only concerned with Dodson and on top of that, he was drunk. A Mexican, any Mexican, wouldn't be a priority in the man's mind.

Murphy untied the sorrel's reins, checked the latigo, and mounted. He had intended to spend the night in Tucson, but now all he wanted to do was find a trough, water the horse, and leave.

The buggy and Vera Cruz were his next stop, some eighty miles to the south and a little east. Oddly, considering the day's long ride, he wasn't sleepy and the night would make for cooler going.

The sorrel trotted down the street, immediately reminding Murphy of why he hated him.

CHAPTER 4

MURPHY AWOKE TO a knock on the door. He raised up on the bed and looked around the small room, wondering where he was.

Then he remembered. He was in a hotel room in Vera Cruz. After leaving Tucson he had ridden through the night. When daylight came, he was worn out and ready to sleep, but the shadeless desert and hot sun prevented it, so he traveled on.

At the site where his map showed the buggy should have been, he searched for hours without finding the faintest trace of hoof or wheel. Late last night he arrived in Vera Cruz. A boy had met him at the livery stable, helped him care for the sorrel, and brought him to this hotel, saying it was the best and cheapest in town.

The knock came again, louder than before. Murphy reluctantly threw his feet to the floor and stood. Except for his boots and gun belt, he was fully dressed, having been too tired to remove his clothes last night. He pulled the .44 Smith from the holster that hung on a bed post and stepped to the door.

"Who is it?"

"It is I. Gabriel."

Gabriel? Murphy opened the door. The boy he had met last night at the livery walked in and plopped down on the end of the bed as if he owned the room.

"It is bad for you to sleep all day, señor. I have given your horse more oats, brushed him, cleaned his hooves, and polished your saddle so hard it shines like new. I waited for you but you did not come out. Tell me what it is you want and I will go and get it."

Murphy couldn't help but grin. He shut the door, staring in amazement at the gangling barefooted youngster who couldn't be much more than eleven or twelve years old. The kid was bolder than anyone Murphy had ever met and completely at ease despite the fact he was standing in front of a man he hardly knew who had a gun in his hand. Murphy holstered the Smith, put his gun belt on, and went to the window, opening the curtain a bit.

"What time is it?"

"It is almost noon. You sleep too much." Gabriel picked up Murphy's boots. "You should let me polish these. I will not charge you too much. They will shine and the señoritas will take notice of you. Would you like for me to get you a woman?"

"That's okay," Murphy said, chuckling. He didn't know why, but he liked this kid and was enjoying his company. "How much you figure I owe you for tending to my horse and polishing my saddle, which I don't remember hiring you to do?"

"Not too much. One dollar."

Murphy's eyes narrowed. Border towns were always full of streetwise, often orphaned kids like Gabriel who were continually watching for the next rich gringo to ride in. A dollar was nearly a full day's wage for most men.

He reached into his pocket and flipped the boy a quarter. "Guess that'll have to do, or you're fired."

Gabriel took a worn leather pouch from his rear pocket and put the coin in it. His large brown eyes were bright and showed no resentment at the sudden steep reduction in his asked wages.

He handed Murphy his boots. "It is not enough, but I will work for you a while longer. Do you want me to bring you a bottle of tequila? Maybe you want me to get you something to eat?"

A thought struck Murphy as he took his hat off a peg on the wall. "Gabriel, you ever know a Santiago Villabisencio?"

"Of course I know him, Sheriff. Everyone here knows he and his sons were attacked by bandits and they are missing. Señor Villabisencio's buggy is at the livery."

Murphy glanced at the saddlebags on top of the dresser, stepped over to Gabriel, and took hold of his arm. "Why did you call me sheriff?"

Gabriel looked down and Murphy raised him off the bed. "Answer me, boy. You've been in my saddlebags, haven't you?"

"I only looked. I did not take the badge. It is still there."

Murphy released his grip, went to the saddlebags, and checked the contents. One pair of binoculars, three pairs of handcuffs, one box of 210-grain .40-.60s for his Winchester, a box of .44s for his pistol, a few pieces of jerky, a hunting knife, and the badge. Nothing appeared to be missing.

Murphy's temper quickly dwindled and he turned to Gabriel, who was watching him as apprehensively as a whipped pup. To further scold the scruffy-haired boy would not do any good. He hadn't stolen anything, which was surprising, and his curiosity no doubt came naturally, considering the life he led.

Yet at least for now, Murphy didn't want his occupation known. There was no telling where this trail was going to take him, and he might be able to gather more information if everyone thought he was just another drifter passing through.

"Tell you what," Murphy spoke softly. "I'll make you a deal. You don't tell anyone I'm a lawman, and when I'm through here, I'll give you my binoculars . . . the badge too. I've got another one in my desk drawer back in Turrett."

Gabriel beamed. "I will not tell. I am very good at not telling. But why do you not want anyone to know? To be a sheriff is a good thing. I would like to be a sheriff. I would wear a gun like yours, maybe two guns, and I would walk up and down the road so everyone could see me."

"I believe you would, at that." Murphy almost laughed. "But some people don't like the law and I don't have any authority here anyway. Let's just you and me keep it a secret for now."

"I will not tell. One time I worked for a deputy marshal, you know. He paid me a lot of money."

"He did, huh? What'd you do for him?"

"Whatever he wanted. I am very good at finding out things. Whatever happens here, I know about it. You should think about hiring me all the time."

Murphy wondered how much of what Gabriel said was true, deciding it might be considerably more than anyone would think. He opened the door.

"You coming?"

"Where are we going?"

"To eat. After that, you're going to show me Santiago's buggy."

Gabriel spoke enthusiastically as he headed out the door. "I will be fair with you, señor. I will not charge you *too* much. You are lucky you found me."

Eating took a lot longer than Murphy thought it would, because Gabriel insisted that there was only one cafe in Vera Cruz worth going to and it was on the west side of town. The food was good, Murphy had to admit, and the price was right. Of course the fact that the small, three-table establishment served ice cream couldn't have been the reason Gabriel wanted to go there. The boy ate three bowlsful on top of a heaping plate of beans and cornbread.

Afterward, at the livery, Murphy learned from the stable hand that a family passing through in a wagon had seen the abandoned buggy and had tied it behind them, bringing it into town.

Murphy inspected the buggy carefully, hoping to find a slug buried somewhere in the woodwork that would reveal the caliber of the weapon used in the assault. He couldn't find a single bullet hole. The bloodstains Risa had told him about were still on the seats, telling him nothing he didn't already know.

With a despondent feeling, Murphy left the livery and ambled slowly down the street. He knew of several murders and mysterious disappearances that had never been solved. Fortunately none of these had occurred inside his jurisdiction, except one, which came awfully close to remaining unsolved.

An elderly Irishman had a rock shack in the foothills north of Turrett. He also had a good spring on his homestead, which he used to irrigate a small garden and orchard. One day a trapper happened by and found the old man dead with a bullet in his head. The trapper reported it and helped Murphy bury the badly decomposed body.

Most everyone in Turrett County believed a nearby rancher who had long coveted the Irishman's water was responsible, but the accusation couldn't be proved. Months went by while Murphy exhausted every possible lead. He had just about given up when he stopped in the saloon one night for a beer and sat at a corner table in the back.

Soon two drunk cowboys came in and parked themselves at the bar. One of them started bragging to the bartender about what a fine shot the other one was, stating that he had seen him hit a coyote in the head at three hundred yards and that the old Irishman had been a lot farther than that. Murphy promptly arrested the both of them, and by morning he had the suspected rancher, who had hired the murderer, in custody.

Murphy reflected on how sometimes the outlook on a

case could change in a hurry. He started to feel a bit more optimistic. Risa's allegation that Ben King was responsible for her husband's and sons' disappearance wasn't much, but it was the only lead he had, and King did have the motive.

But riding out to King's ranch now and confronting him would be stupid. King certainly wouldn't admit to anything, and if he was indeed responsible, the action would only bolster his guard. There had to be other ways to investigate the cattleman without arousing his suspicion.

Right now, Murphy concluded, the biggest question he faced wasn't who may have committed the assault, but where were the victims that showed a crime had been committed? After being missing for so long, Santiago and his sons were almost certainly dead, yet it would be impossible to prove even that in a court of law without the corpses. The killer, or killers, must have known that. That's why they took the bodies and disposed of them.

Murphy stopped under the shady overhang of a store and rolled a cigarette. To him, the blood on the buggy seats definitely spelled foul play, but a defense attorney worth his salt would explain it away as possibly coming from a cut finger, hand, or even a bloody nose.

And then there were the missing buggy horses. Why were they taken? Anyone would know that possession of those horses would implicate them. Murphy believed he had the answer. The horses were needed to carry the three victims off. Afterward, they were either killed and buried or burned, or, more likely, they were taken across the border into Mexico and sold.

A small whirlwind kicked up dust in the street, and for the first time since leaving the livery, Murphy took note of his surroundings. Gabriel was standing at a busy street corner ahead, waiting expectantly for him to catch up. The rock, adobe, and clapboard buildings couldn't have been built more than a few months ago.

Murphy stopped alongside his newfound young friend. Gabriel gestured to the side of a row of saloons and brothels. "This is Pine Street. You want to get into a fight, or you want to drink or have a woman, this is where you come. I know everybody here. Here is where everything happens."

"I can see that," Murphy said, surprised at how many horses, buggies, and wagons lined the street in the middle of the day. "Why are all these buildings new? Did they just build this section of town?"

"Oh no, señor. There was a big fire. It took away everything, but they rebuilded it very quickly. You want for me to take you around? Like I told you, I know everyone."

"That would be—"

A gunshot came from down the street. Then another. Several riders appeared at a gallop. They were cowboys, Murphy guessed, coming to town to have a little fun for possibly the first time in months. They'd get drunk, visit the prostitutes, and leave when their money ran out, which usually didn't take long.

Once in a while, especially after the fall roundup, cowhands like these had ridden into Turrett. Murphy generally left them alone as long as they halfway behaved themselves.

The four cowboys yelled and fired a few more shots in the air. They were almost straight across from Murphy, running their horses fast, when a frightened donkey pulling a straw-laden, two-wheeled carreta broke loose from its Mexican master and trotted into their path.

One rider and horse hit the ass broadside. Both animals and the cowboy went down hard. Another horse plowed into the carreta, and a third jumped it, skimming a pile of straw off the top.

Dust boiled up. The donkey scrambled to its feet, and the heavyset Mexican ran to grab the animal's lead rope. When he had it, he started pulling on the donkey, trying to leave.

The cowboy who had managed to avoid the wreck wheeled his bay mare around, shook out his lariat, and in two swings settled the loop tightly around the Mexican's neck.

Then he dallied, put his spurs to the mare, and viciously yanked the brown-robed man to the ground.

Murphy didn't want to interfere, didn't want to get into a fight on his first day in Vera Cruz, yet he couldn't bring himself to allow the Mexican to be dragged to death in the street.

He shouted. "Turn him loose! Get your rope off the saddle horn!"

The thin-faced, mustached cowboy spun the mare to face Murphy, but made no move to unwrap the dally.

"I mean it," Murphy said, his voice quieter. "We don't have to have any trouble here. Just turn him loose."

To the side Murphy saw the rider who had been thrown get shakily to his feet. Blood streamed from his nose and mixed with the dirt on his face and dripped off his chin. He limped a step forward, gesturing at the prone Mexican while looking at Murphy.

"Mister, I don't know what part you think you got in this, but you'd be smart to start walkin' and get clean out of the way. That greaser and his jackass dang near got us all killed, and we're sure goin' to teach him a lesson by lettin' him gurgle on the end of a rope a while."

Another rider, the one who had jumped the carreta, trotted a flashy black stud alongside the cowhand holding the rope. He was young, hardly in his twenties, if that, straw-haired, and wore a two-gun rig on his hips. Murphy intuitively recognized a dangerous recklessness about him and realized that if gunplay erupted, it was likely to start there.

Without taking his eyes off the men, Murphy stepped to the side and in front of Gabriel, pushing him backward with his body. "Go on, kid, leave. You'll get hurt."

The man with the bloody face spoke again. "It ain't that greaser kid you need to be worryin' about, mister. You done bit off a heap more'n you can chew. We're givin' you one last chance to turn around and mind your own business."

Murphy didn't move. The cowboy whose horse had struck the carreta was up and walking his way. Four men, four guns. The odds were against him. It seemed to Murphy like they had always been against him.

He wanted to talk to the men, tell them that they shouldn't have been shooting and running their horses in the street and that the accident was as much their fault as it was the Mexican's. Yet he knew it wouldn't do any good. He had braced them, and their pride was at stake. One side or the other had to back down, and Murphy couldn't. Wouldn't.

He slowly moved his right hand closer to the butt of the Smith. "You may get me, but I'm not going anywhere alone."

Murphy glared at the man holding the rope, at the same time watching the hands of the young mounted cowboy beside him. "When I count to three that rope had better be off your saddle horn.

"One."

A half dozen bystanders had gathered along the street to watch. Murphy was unaware of their presence.

Foolishness. Murphy almost spoke the word out loud. Someone was going to die over nothing but pure foolishness. Men weren't much above animals. Not much.

"Two."

Murphy's voice was loud in the stillness, steady. Sweat beaded the cowboy's face and his hands trembled noticeably. This man, Murphy surmised, was no gunfighter. He was just a cowboy who had come to town to enjoy himself and was now caught up in a melee from which there was no easy escape.

The Mexican lay facedown in the dusty street, motionless.

"Thr . . ."

The cowboy swung open his dally and dropped the rope. The reckless young fellow beside him, mounted on the black stud, went for his left gun.

He drew quicker than Murphy, had his revolver aimed sooner, but the time it took him to pull the hammer back on the Colt broke even with Murphy's trigger pull on the double-action Smith.

The guns boomed together as if only one shot had been fired. Murphy felt a sting on the top of his right shoulder. He had clasped the Smith in both hands and started to pull the trigger again when he saw his target fall limply out of the saddle.

Another shot came and Murphy instinctively dropped to the ground and rolled. He came up in a crouch and fired at the bloody-faced man. The man's gun went off, striking the earth a few feet in front of him, and he staggered a long moment, blood spurting out of a bullet hole just above his heart. Then he fell.

The cowboy whose horse had hit the carreta started running, and the one who had roped the Mexican had both hands high in the air.

Murphy stood up. A sickening feeling came over him, a filthy feeling that made him turn and slowly walk away from what he had done. There were men who needed killing, but these didn't seem to be that kind. It had all been a mistake. One big, horrible mistake.

Gabriel soon caught up with Murphy and tugged on his shirt sleeve. "I saw everything, señor. You were magnificent. Never have I seen anything like it. You could have shot all four of them."

"Look, Gabriel." Murphy stopped and faced him. "There's nothing magnificent about killing someone. You live with it always, always wondering if there was something you could have done different than what you did."

"But you should not feel bad, señor. I know those men. They are from el señor King's rancho. They would have killed the padre. I know they would have. They have hung Mexican and Chinese people here before."

Murphy was startled to learn that the owner of the donkey was a priest and that the four cowboys worked for Ben King. How would King take the death of two of his hands? Would there be retaliation? And what effect would the fight have on his ability to gather information about Santiago's disappearance?

"Señor," Gabriel broke Murphy's thoughts. "You are bleeding badly. You should come with me. I know a man who is very good at fixing people. He will not charge you too much."

Murphy glanced at his shoulder, surprised at the large bloodstain on his shirt. There was hardly any pain from the wound.

"All right, Gabriel. I think maybe you were right—I am lucky to have found you."

CHAPTER 5

AT NIGHT, VERA Cruz's Pine Street was at least twice as busy as it had been in the day. In the space of a block, Murphy counted six saloons, and every hitching rail was full.

The hour was late. Murphy had spent some time lying on the bed in his hotel room before concluding that, at least for a while, sleep was unattainable.

His shoulder wound had turned out to be little more than a scratch, and the Chinese physician Gabriel had taken him to had done a good job bandaging it. Afterward, he had gone by the town marshal's office to report his version of the shooting, but the marshal wasn't in.

Murphy crossed the street, finally deciding to enter one of the busy establishments and hopefully find an empty table in the back where he could sip a beer, watch, and listen.

He looked inside three of the saloons before going in one that appeared to have enough room for him. It was a nicer place than the others, polished mahogany bar, large mirrors, carpet, a couple of chandeliers, and the drinks were no doubt more expensive.

Murphy stepped up to the bar and ordered a beer. When he started to pay for it, a hand touched his arm. "Your money's no good here, friend."

A tall, thick-bearded man dressed in a pin-striped suit was beside Murphy. He nodded at the bartender. "Give him whatever he wants and put the bill on my tab."

The man took a step back and offered to shake. "Name's Walcott. Harry Walcott. I'm sort of the recently designated mayor of Vera Cruz and I saw what happened in the street today. You're the kind of man this town needs. That cowboy riffraff have been running roughshod over everyone for way too long."

Murphy shook Walcott's hand, noticing the man's thick waist and double chin. He raised the beer. "Thanks."

Harry waved his hand to show that the gratitude was unnecessary. He reached into his coat pocket, pulled out a long silver case, and offered Murphy a cigar.

"I don't mean to pry, but I haven't seen you in town before. Will you be staying long?"

"Could be." Murphy took a drink. The beer was cold, good.

"You wouldn't happen to be interested in a job, would you?"

Murphy struck a match with his thumbnail and lit the cigar. He hadn't considered looking for work in Vera Cruz, or anywhere else for that matter. He had a job waiting on him in Turrett.

Nevertheless, the idea was intriguing. There was no way of knowing how long he'd have to be here, and although he had enough money to last several weeks, it would eventually run out. Then, too, if the job Harry was talking about was here in the saloon, it would be a hard place to beat when it came to finding out things.

"What did you have in mind?"

Walcott blew out a thick puff of smoke. "Vera Cruz is growing extremely fast. There are nine major silver mines in operation in the area and at least a dozen smaller producing claims. But like any young boomtown, it is fast filling with racketeers, gunmen, horse thieves, prostitutes, and gamblers who see it only as a chance to cash in on lawlessness before the good people of the area can establish churches, schools, and a strong government.

"Vera Cruz needs a resourceful, intelligent, and efficient man like you to fill the office of city marshal. The pay is better than anything else you can find in the territory. One hundred dollars a week, and with your approval I think I can have your appointment confirmed by noon to-morrow."

Intelligent. Resourceful. Efficient. Murphy thought Walcott would make a good snake-oil salesman. The man knew nothing about him. The offer, however, was amazingly good. Murphy's sheriff's pay at Turrett was barely a fourth of that, and he was responsible for an entire county. A hardworking miner didn't make over two to three dollars a day, and field and ranch hands made about half that.

The money was tempting and Murphy couldn't help but consider it. If he was careful, in a year he could save as much as four thousand dollars. That was enough to buy a good little ranch, house and livestock included. Or maybe a gun shop or mercantile. He wouldn't have to run it; he could hire a clerk.

And being a lawman was the only thing he'd ever found that he was good at. Vera Cruz would be a challenge, and the high salary was doubtless due to the job's hazards and the civic leaders' inability to fill the position, yet Turrett and Cincherville had had their rough moments, too.

Still, he liked his job in Turrett, liked his friends, and the small town had become his home.

"Well"—Walcott brushed the ashes of his cigar in an ash-tray on the bar—"are you interested?"

Murphy continued to contemplate, taking a long, slow sip of beer. He had told Gabriel to keep quiet about his being a lawman in the hope that the less attention he drew, the easier it might be to gain information without creating suspicion. Now, because of the shooting incident, Ben King, along with the whole town, would be watching him.

He might just as well be wearing a badge; it could actually put him in a better position to continue his investigation of Santiago's disappearance. While his official authority would end at the edge of town, his title would have weight with other territorial officials and officers, perhaps even Marshal Dodson.

"Tell you what, Mr. Walcott." Murphy set his beer down. "I've had a little experience in this kind of work and I'll take the job on the condition that everything is done my way, no arguments. The first change I'll enforce is that no one is allowed to carry a gun in town but me. I want a hundred and fifty dollars a week and a deputy of my choosing, who will cost you another seventy-five. There will be times when I'll need to be gone a few days and I don't want any grumbling over it."

"Well . . . I don't know?" Harry scratched his chin. "I don't think the town can afford that much."

"What happened to your last marshal?" Murphy asked.

"Uh, he was killed a few weeks ago. Shot in the back."

"I'm not asking for too much then, am I, Mr. Walcott? Looks to me like I may not be asking for enough."

Harry stuck his cigar in the corner of his mouth. "You do have a point." He pulled out his pocket watch. "I'd better be going. I have an appointment. I'll let you know by tomorrow. Where are you staying?"

"The Plaza Hotel."

"Fine. It was nice meeting you and I'll be in touch."

Murphy watched Walcott leave. He believed there was a good chance the town leaders would find him too independent and expensive, and if so, perhaps that was for the best. He would be taking on an awful lot of trouble, and like earlier today, he usually managed to get into enough of that without looking for it.

After drinking another beer, Murphy went to his hotel room and lay down. In the morning, whether he got the job or not, he'd write Risa a note telling her where he was and what he was doing. Then he'd get Gabriel to help him hire someone to take the note, buggy, and borrowed sorrel horse to San Patricio, returning to Vera Cruz with the dun.

And he should get a letter off to the two deputies he had left in charge at Turrett. It didn't look like he would be heading for home any time soon.

CHAPTER 6

THE JULY AFTERNOON was hot. Murphy set the sawed-off, double-barreled 16-gauge Greener shotgun he had taken from the marshal's office against the edge of the board-walk, took a hammer from his back pocket, and tacked a notice on the veranda's support post.

Gabriel, who had been with Murphy most of the day, stepped closer. "What does the paper say?"

"It says," Murphy tried to keep a straight face, " 'Wanted for mischief. Small Mexican boy approximately five feet tall, dark hair, and brown eyes. Subject last seen in Vera Cruz using the alias Gabriel. Five-hundred-dollar reward.' "

"It does not say that," Gabriel said, smiling. "I am not a Mexican, you know. I am an Apache."

Murphy looked at him. The boy did have the features of most of the Apaches he had seen. Wide, heavy cheeks, thin lips, and a round, small-nosed face.

"What makes you think you're an Indian?" he asked.

"A padre at the mission in Tucson where I stayed told me."

"What were you doing at a mission in Tucson?"

"Someone took me there when I was very little. I do not know who it was. The padre taught me how to speak Spanish and English. He was very old and he died. A year, or maybe it was two years ago, I ran away from there and came to here so I could make a lot of money."

"You don't have any folks, relatives?"

Gabriel shook his head. A moment later his face brightened. "I think maybe I am the grandson of Cochise."

"How do you figure that?"

"It is because I am an Apache. Chochise and his woman probably had a lot of babies and then those babies had more babies. I am one of them."

"Sounds good to me."

Gabriel touched the paper. "What does it really say?"

Murphy put the hammer back in his pocket, picked up the shotgun and began to read. " 'By order of the city marshal—' "

"That is you," Gabriel interrupted. "You know I have not told anyone that you are a sheriff and you promised to me your badge and binoculars?"

"Well, it doesn't make much difference now whether anyone knows or not, and I said I'd give them to you when I left. I haven't left yet, have I?"

"No. But you might forget to do it."

"I won't forget." Murphy looked at the notice and continued reading. " 'No firearms of any kind shall be carried by any person within the limits of Vera Cruz. Check all guns in at the marshal's office or at the Homestake Saloon.' "

"You have a gun and you are a person," Gabriel pointed out.

"I'm also the marshal."

"They will not do it, you know."

"Who won't do what, Gabriel?"

"The cowboys. They will not give their guns to you."

"Yes, they will."

"No, they will not. They—"

"Gabriel," Murphy's voice was sharp. "You've been hanging around me all day. Go and find something else to do."

"You want me to find someone else to work for?"

"Yeah. That's a good idea. Go do that."

"I will leave then. Someone else might pay me a lot more money. Maybe I will work for them all the time."

"It's a free country. Like everybody else, you got a right to make all you can."

Gabriel started walking and Murphy called to him. "Meet you about dark to buy your supper."

The boy turned, smiling. "And ice cream?"

"Yeah, that too."

Murphy finished posting the notices around town and returned to his office to clean out the desk and go through a large, oak filing cabinet beside it.

Walcott had given him the job of city marshal, along with the salary and conditions he had asked for, a little before noon, less than three hours ago. The small rock jail had two cells in the back and a metal cot against one wall of the office.

By nightfall, Murphy intended to have the place cleaned up and be moved in. There was no use in wasting money on a hotel room when he had everything he needed here, and since it might take a while to find a good deputy, he'd have to guard and care for any prisoners himself.

Running footsteps sounded on the plank boardwalk in front of the jail, and a man wearing a white apron rushed through the open door. A trickle of blood was coming from the corner of his mouth as he spoke between heaving breaths.

"Marshal, you'd better get over to the Homestake. There's a miner in there with a shooter. I told him about the new law, that he had to check his gun in. He just hit me with the back of his hand and laughed."

Murphy rose from his chair, took the Greener shotgun from the gun rack on the wall, and headed outside with the bartender following him close behind. He knew when he had posted the ordinance it would take the town and the people in the surrounding area some time to adjust to it, but he hadn't expected any trouble until tonight when the miners and cowboys were off work.

He reached the saloon and peered above the bat-wing doors. One man, a very big man, dressed in denim trousers, suspenders, and a dusty red flannel shirt was standing at the bar with his back to Murphy. He was waving a bottle in his left hand while talking loudly to a couple of patrons seated at a table.

Murphy stepped quietly inside and leveled the Greener on him without pulling the hammers back. If at all possible, he had no intention of using the deadly weapon. He only carried it for its intimidating effect.

The move drew the attention of the men at the table, and in a moment the huge man quit talking and turned around. He looked even bigger from the front, with flat, angular shoulders that were so wide most any two men could stand side by side between them.

He had a scruffy black beard, little ears pinned flat against a round skull, and a thick, short neck that looked almost like an extension of his shoulders. His muscular brown arms were so long his hands nearly reached his knees.

He took a drink and threw the bottle against the bar, breaking it. "I see that weasel barkeep hidin' behind you. Well, that badge and pepper-shooter you're a-totin' don't mean nothin' to me. You and him want my smoke pole, you come on and get it. Ain't nobody ever whipped me and you two won't neither."

"I don't want to fight you," Murphy said, meaning every word. "All I want is the same thing I'm asking everyone in town to do. Check your gun in until you leave. There's been too many killings in Vera Cruz, and I want them stopped."

The miner tapped the hardwood grip on the pistol tucked in his waistband. "Like I said. You want it, you come and get it."

Murphy was in a dilemma. He had to get the gun or his credibility as city marshal would be ruined his first day on the job. Yet he didn't want a shooting. That left just one alternative, and he dreaded it worse than anything he'd come across in years. He had to fight this giant, had to somehow beat him and take the pistol.

He stepped closer, turning the Greener sideways in his hands. If he could jab the butt of the shotgun in the miner's gut and knock the wind out of him, he might have a chance. *Might.*

The move was sudden, unexpected, and Murphy hit him with all the strength he could muster. The miner grunted and doubled over, clutching his middle.

Murphy knew he must act quickly to keep the big man from catching his breath. He took the muzzle end of the shotgun in both hands and swung the barrel like a bat. There was a heavy thud and a loud snap when the stock on the Greener broke, half of it falling to the floor in splinters. The blow struck the miner's side hard, and he jerked up and twisted from it, sucking air with a loud gasp.

Voices came from behind and the saloon doors flapped open. Murphy didn't look long at the two customers who stepped inside, a few seconds at most, but it was enough time for the miner to gather his tremendous power, spread his arms, and lunge for him.

He tried to avoid those long arms. He jumped backward and ducked, but a hand caught his shirt at the collar and yanked him upright as if he were made of straw. The miner wrapped his arms around Murphy and used his weight to slam him against the edge of the bar.

Pain shot through Murphy. His vision blurred, and now he was the one who couldn't breathe. The miner picked him up in a bear hug, grunted, and squeezed. The shotgun slipped from his fingers. He felt like he was in a huge, steel vise and it was only a matter of time until it crushed him to pieces.

Murphy fought desperately to break free. He struggled and kicked with everything in him, yet his efforts had no effect. A light-headed, dizzy feeling washed over him and along with it came the realization that he would pass out soon. After that, if this brute didn't release him, he would die.

The miner's chin was resting on the top of Murphy's

head, and in one last attempt at freedom, Murphy sank his teeth deep into the man's throat. The result was immediate. At first the miner cried out in a low, guttural tone and squeezed harder, then his grip faded until at last he dropped his arms and pushed Murphy away.

Murphy fell to the floor. Blood was in his mouth and smeared around it. He lay there taking in great gulps of air. When his vision began to clear, he could see the miner standing above him.

Fierce anger stormed through Murphy, giving him strength. He had gotten into this fight because he didn't want to use his gun, didn't want another killing on his hands. That streak of decency had nearly cost him his life.

Still breathing hard, he pulled the Smith from his holster, pointed it at the miner, and slowly made it to his feet. "This game's over, mister. I want your gun and I want it now."

The miner took his hand from his throat, revealing a nasty, bloody, bite wound close to his jugular. He touched his side. "You busted a coupla my ribs with that scattergun of yours, but I told ya you couldn't whip me. You ain't nothin' but another yellow-bellied, egg-suckin' law dog like every other one I ever seen. Without that badge and six-shooter, you ain't nothin', nothin' atall."

Murphy's anger changed to reckless, uncontrollable fury. This arrogant giant needed to be beaten, had to be beaten. He holstered the Smith, unbuckled his gun belt, and laid it on the bar. "All right," he said, taking a step closer to the big man. "You want a fight, you'll get one."

A smile formed on the miner's lips and Murphy swung, hitting him squarely on the jaw with his right fist. The blow popped like a small-caliber gunshot, and the man shook his head, staring in disbelief. Murphy wasted no time. He hit him again in the same spot, followed by a left hook to the nose.

The miner raised his arms and charged, but Murphy

sidestepped the move easily and hit him hard in his broken ribs. The giant groaned like a wounded grizzly and turned. Murphy was waiting for him, and he threw all of his weight behind a roundhouse right to the stomach. The punch seemed to have little effect, and Murphy quickly withdrew to keep away from his opponent's groping hands.

So far, the fight was going well for Murphy. The miner either didn't want to use his fists or knew he was too slow to hit anything with them. Yet the punishing blows that would have already sent many a lesser man to the floor had had minimal results. The miner's stance was as sturdy as ever, and except for a bloody nose, there was no change in him.

Murphy's biggest worry was to make sure he continued to keep his distance. If the man were able to get hold of him again and turn their quarrel into a wrestling match, there would be no escape, no chance.

Cautiously, Murphy circled his burly adversary. The knuckles on his right fist were already bruised and torn, and it was questionable how long he would be able to continue to strike the man. Somehow, and fairly soon, he had to find a way to end it.

The miner took a step toward him. Murphy faked a right, jumped to the left, and swung his right again, landing it full in the man's eye. Then he wound behind him, hitting him once behind the ear.

An idea came to Murphy. He might spend all day hammering away at this human tree and do nothing but wear himself out. He needed to concentrate on a specific area— like the eyes. If he could get them so swollen the man couldn't see, he could finish him.

In what seemed to be an eternity to Murphy, but was actually less than fifteen minutes, he stepped back several feet from his opponent and tried to catch his breath. His arms felt like they were sticks of jelly, and his hands were so battered and sore he could hardly flex them. Most of the tables in the room were overturned, and the place was now full of spectators.

Twice the miner had nearly gotten a grip on him before he could wriggle free. His shirt was in shreds, and there were long, deep scratch marks on his back and neck.

Murphy watched the miner flounder about blindly. Where his eyes should have been were two swollen mounds of ugly, purplish, broken flesh.

"I still want your shooter," Murphy said loudly. "You about had enough?"

The big man made a short charge at Murphy's voice, stopping when he was unable to locate him. "I'm still standin', ain't I? You ain't whipped ole Sam Bundy yet."

Murphy moved to the bar and strapped on his gun belt. The fight was over. He wasn't about to keep pounding on a blind man. There remained only one thing left to do.

He slipped quietly behind the miner, took the Smith from his holster, and struck him on the back of the head with the butt of it. The giant wheeled, staggered a moment, then fell. Murphy holstered his gun, bent over the unconscious man, and removed the pistol from his waistband. Then he looked for what was left of the Greener, found it, and started for the door.

Several men who had been watching were standing in the way and they moved, making an aisle for him to pass. No one spoke, and except for the shuffle of his feet, the saloon was quiet.

He stepped outside. A breeze was blowing, carrying a faint scent of rain, and a few dark thunderclouds hung low in the sky. Murphy looked down the street and saw a group of riders approaching. Presently they reined their horses alongside the hitching rail in front of him; he noted they were all wearing guns.

Before any of them had the chance to dismount, thereby making it difficult for him to watch them all at once, he stepped to the edge of the boardwalk.

"Listen up, men," Murphy called loudly. "I'm the new city marshal, and firearms are no longer allowed in Vera Cruz. You can check your sidearms inside and pick them up when you leave. I want you to have a good time, but there'll be no gunplay in town unless it's mine."

One of the cowboys, a man who looked faintly familiar, nudged his horse closer to a much older central rider. He pointed at Murphy. "That's him. He's the one who shot George and Johnny, 'cept he wasn't wearin' no badge then."

The older man, who could have been anywhere from fifty to sixty, loomed broad and heavy in the saddle. He was strongly grizzled about the temples, with a wide, thin mouth under a silver-gray tobacco-stained mustache, and his small, beaked nose looked oddly out of place between puffy, veined cheeks.

He had an air of authority about him, and he glared at Murphy with a pair of gray-green eyes that carried an impact difficult to face.

"So you're the back-shootin' newcomer who shot my men. I'll bet the scared rabbits in this town didn't waste any time pinning that badge on you, did they? Probably paying you real good, too. But you won't enjoy none of it, won't live long enough to. I'll see to that."

"What's your name?" Murphy asked. He thought he knew but wanted to make sure.

"Ben King, and it's a name you aren't likely to forget. I own just about everything around here except for this sorry excuse for a town. It won't be long until I'll own it too."

Murphy realized this confrontation could easily escalate into a gun battle. Besides the fact that he intended to disarm these men, their sole purpose in being here was likely to kill him. His only hope was to get the drop on them with the broken-stocked Greener.

He covered King with the shotgun. The thought occurred to him to corner the rancher about the disappearance of Santiago and his sons, but he quickly dismissed the idea. Talk on the subject would just put King on his guard and wouldn't accomplish anything.

He forced his swollen, bloody right hand to pull back one of the hammers. "Mr. King, an important man like you is always welcome in Vera Cruz. But I'll have your guns, or you and your men won't be staying."

King gestured at his cowboys. "I guess you really think you can take all seven of us?"

"No," Murphy managed to cock the other hammer on the Greener with his left hand while keeping his index finger on his right through the trigger guard. "I'll only get two, and you'll be one of them."

For a long moment King's eyes shifted from Murphy's to the large, twin bores of the shotgun. He was a man used to giving orders, not taking them, and it rankled him to have to back down in front of his men. Yet Murphy was too calm, too sure. He would shoot, King was certain of it.

King wheeled his horse. "Come on, boys. I have an idea this town will get friendlier in a few days, a whole lot friendlier."

CHAPTER 7

MURPHY LEANED AGAINST the livery corral rails watching the dun chomp on the pile of hay he had thrown him. The young stable hand he and Gabriel had hired to return Pena's sorrel and Risa's buggy to San Patricio had returned with the dun yesterday, and Murphy was glad to have the horse back. Sometime in the near future he planned to take a ride and do some snooping around. The bodies of Santiago, Froylan, and Antonio had to be somewhere.

The dun snorted softly and Murphy pushed himself away from the fence so he could reach in his pocket for his cigarette makings. Three days had passed since his fight with the miner, and although the swelling in his hands had gone down, they were still sore.

Word about the fight and his altercation with Ben King had spread rapidly, and he hadn't had any more problems with the enforcement of his new firearms policy. The various shop, saloon, and gambling house owners in town seemed happy with him, speaking or waving as he made his rounds, yet Murphy didn't trust them. They were his friends as long as he did what they wanted and helped to protect their business interests.

Outside of that, they could care less, and he didn't believe a single one of them would lift a finger to help him if he lay dying in the street. He was alone here in Arizona, and perhaps that was for the best. No one to count on meant no one to depend on and it forced a man to rely only on himself.

A sound came from behind Murphy, the almost inaudible sound of footsteps, and his move was automatic, involuntary. He dropped the cigarette papers and tobacco in his hand, ducked low and whirled, pulling the Smith in one blurred motion. He leveled the revolver on Gabriel, his finger on the trigger ready to fire double-action.

"It is I," Gabriel said with wide eyes. Murphy holstered the Smith, angry with himself for being so touchy and wasting what would have been a perfectly good smoke. Again he took the makings from his pocket.

"Quit sneaking around, Gabriel. One of these days it's going to get you in trouble."

"I was not sneaking."

"Yes, you were. Speak out when you're walking up to somebody's back."

"If you want, I will speak, but I was not sneaking."

Murphy gently rolled the tobacco-filled cigarette paper between his fingers, raised it to his mouth, and licked the edge. After he lit it and took a puff, Gabriel stepped closer.

"I made the jail to shine, you know. I have been working very hard for a long time. You do not owe me too much. I think two dollars."

"Two dollars!" Murphy had learned that Gabriel asked a dollar for just about everything he did and after negotiations he usually settled for from a fourth to half of that, but *two* dollars?

"Gabriel, you're a robber. A miniature pirate. No, you're . . . you're a professional con man, that's what you are. I'm not paying you any two dollars for cleaning my office."

"You come and see. I worked very hard. I broomed the floor and mopped it. And I broomed the walls and window and washed it. I put clean water in the pail for you to wash your face and hands in, and I made the jail to smell very good. I think maybe I should charge you more money. Two dollars is a very cheap price."

"Sure it is, Gabriel. It's only enough to hire two full-grown men to work from sunup till dark."

Gabriel's face was blank, unreadable, and Murphy couldn't help but smile at the boy's gall.

"Well, let's go see what makes you think your labor is worth so darned much."

They walked down the street and up on the boardwalk in front of the jail. Gabriel gestured at it in a sweeping motion. "See, I broomed this too."

A strong, flowery smelling odor was coming from inside as Murphy moved closer to the door. "This place smells like a cathouse. Where'd you steal the perfume, Gabriel?"

"I did not steal it. A woman, she owed me a lot of money and she gave it to me. It smells very good, don't you think?"

"How much of it did you use?"

"It was not a very big bottle. I put some on your desk and on your blanket and on your pillow. I think I forgot to charge you for it."

"On my pillow?" Murphy stepped inside. The evening was waning and only a small amount of light was coming through the window and open door. The stench of perfume was so strong it made his eyes water and nose itch.

"Gabriel!"

"It sure stinks in here, don't it, Marshal?"

Murphy wheeled to see Marshal Dodson sitting behind his desk with his feet propped against the edge, holding an aimed, cocked revolver.

"Don't make me kill you," Dodson said coldly, dropping his feet. "I'd much rather watch you hang in Tucson for murder."

Gabriel walked in and Murphy spoke to him without taking his eyes off the marshal. "Get out of here, kid. Go on. I'll find you later."

Gabriel glanced at Dodson, then hurriedly backed his way out. Murphy briefly considered making a dive for the floor on the chance that Dodson would miss his first shot and give him enough time to draw the Smith. But such a move was too dangerous.

Murphy stood still. "I don't remember having murdered anyone."

"Well, you should." Dodson put both hands around the grip of his Colt. "Less than a week ago you shot two cowhands here in the street. They didn't have an ounce of hardware on between them. Five witnesses are testifying to that fact. They say they saw you shoot those men out of the saddle in cold blood."

Murphy was stunned at the allegation, and it was several moments before he could gather his wits enough to speak. "Several people saw that fight. Both those men drew on me. I've got a scab on the top of my right shoulder where one of their shots grazed me."

"Well that's your word and it's not up to me. A jury will decide. In the meantime I've got a warrant for your arrest signed by the judge in Tucson and I'm taking you there. Drop your gun belt."

Murphy hesitated. His thoughts were spinning as he recounted the shooting on his first full day in Vera Cruz and then, a few days later, his encounter with Ben King outside of the Homestake Saloon. He remembered King's final words and realized this whole thing had to be a setup. The five witnesses Dodson had mentioned were undoubtedly King's men.

Because of his earlier meeting with Dodson in Tucson, Murphy didn't think much of him, yet there was a chance the man was only here in performance of his duties and wasn't a part of the plot.

Dodson stood. "I told you to drop your gun belt. Do it!"

There appeared to be no way out. Murphy slowly unbuckled the belt and let it fall to the floor. "You don't remember me, do you, Dodson?"

"Is there a reason why I should?"

"No, not really. Look, why don't you handcuff me and we'll both go find a man named Harry Walcott. He's the one who hired me as city marshal and he saw the whole incident. I'm sure he can give you the names of a dozen others who saw the shooting. They'll tell you what happened. I shot those two men in self-defense."

"The grand jury already heard all the witnesses they need to. Now turn around and get your hands behind your back."

Murphy complied reluctantly. There was nothing else to do. Even if he could somehow escape, he'd be a wanted man. By going to court, and with the help of a halfway decent defense attorney, it shouldn't be too difficult to clear his name.

One thing now seemed certain. Dodson was more interested in doing King's bidding than he was in seeking justice and upholding the law. And that was likely the reason he hadn't done anything about the disappearance of Santiago and the boys. He already knew who the killer was.

CHAPTER 8

"YOUR MOVE, AL."

The statement broke Murphy's trance and he took his eyes off the early-morning sunlight coming through a window in the corner of the room and looked at the checker game in front of him. He was losing, as usual, but at least the game helped to pass the time.

Because the jail was full, and more than that, because Dodson wanted to make sure his latest prisoner was isolated and given no chance to escape, Murphy had been cooped up for the last two weeks in a temporary cell that was really a small attorney-client briefing room located in the top story of the Tucson courthouse.

His wrists were handcuffed, a ball and chain was attached to his right leg, and except for the late-night hours when he was locked to yet another chain that was fastened to a large eyebolt in the center of the floor, a deputy was posted to constantly guard him.

Deputy Marshal Earl Posey grinned across the table. "I got ya, don't I? You gotta take the jump and when you do, I'm gonna jump three a' yer men. I been linin' up this play for a while and yer done for. You ain't gonna have but one man left against my five, and two of them are done kinged. Ya want to give up and start a new game?"

"You know better than that, Earl," Murphy answered, studying the board. Posey was the deputy Dodson normally assigned to guard him, and Murphy had grown to like the sparely built, homely man. Another deputy who sometimes came, a man named Copeland, treated Murphy with contempt and there was bitterness between them.

A knock sounded at the door and Posey rose from his chair. "Who is it?"

"It's me, Thomas Oberling. I need to speak with my client."

Posey unlocked the door and opened it. "I suppose you two will want to be alone. I'll be right out here in the hall if either of you need me."

Oberling stepped in and closed the door. He was a cadaverously thin man of about forty, dressed in a wine-colored shirt, black tie, black coat, and black trousers. He looked more like the owner and soon-to-be customer of a funeral parlor than he did an attorney.

At first Murphy had objected to the court's appointment of him, preferring instead to hire his own counsel. Later however, after a lengthy visit, Oberling convinced him that he was competent and knowledgeable enough to defend the case. Furthermore, since there were no other attorneys available in the territory outside of Prescott, bringing one in from that far away would be quite time consuming and costly. Oberling thought that a full acquittal of the charges would be easy to obtain without going to that much trouble and expense.

Murphy pushed his chair back. "What brings you here this early, Mister Oberling? Must be something awfully important."

"It is. We're going to trial today."

"Today? I thought it was scheduled for next Tuesday. We can't go to court now. What about our witnesses? We have to have them."

"They are all taken care of. Everything is fine. The jurors have been agreed upon by the prosecution and I, and the testimony should be short and to the point, requiring little to no cross-examination. I expect the jury to begin deliberations this afternoon, returning within an hour or less with their verdict.

"To tell you the truth"—Oberling cleared his throat— "I am glad to get the proceedings over with. My sister, who resides in the East, is violently ill and I plan to catch a train this evening to be with her."

"Not if this trial isn't over," Murphy said flatly. "You're not going anywhere until then."

"Why no, of course not. But it will be. I'm sure of it."

Deputy Marshal Copeland pushed Murphy through the open door of his confinement room, causing him to trip over the iron ball and chain attached to his leg.

Earl Posey caught him by the arm before he fell. "Leave him be, Copeland. He ain't done nothin' to you."

"He's a back-shootin' coward and I got no use for him." Copeland picked up the iron ball and shoved it hard into Murphy's belly. "Carry this and hurry along or I'll drag you into court by the hair on your head."

Murphy gritted his teeth against the anger welling in him and started walking. When the trial was over and he was pronounced a free man, he fully intended to look Copeland up and return at least part of the courtesy the man had shown him.

At the end of the hall they went down a staircase. Due to the shortness of the leg chain, Murphy had to lower the ball each time he took a step with his right foot. The going was slow, and Copeland continually prodded him forward with the muzzle of a Colt shoved in the small of his back.

Finally reaching the ground floor, Posey opened a large, ornately carved oak door, and the three stepped into the small, crowded courtroom. Oberling was sitting alone at a table just outside the spectator railing, and the deputies seated Murphy beside him.

Murphy set the ball on the floor and turned around in his chair, searching for a familiar face from Vera Cruz— like Harry Walcott's. He couldn't find one, but he did see

Ben King and several of his hands sitting on the front row. King gave him a thin, derisive smile, and Murphy shifted around to face Oberling.

"I thought you said everything was fine. I don't recognize a single man here who might be on our side. Where's Walcott?"

"He and the other witnesses from Vera Cruz have been delayed, but I anticipate their arrival at any moment."

"If they don't show up, you ask the judge for a continuance. There's no use letting this show get started without them."

Oberling looked at Murphy coldly. "I am quite capable of doing my job without any advice from you."

The bailiff stepped out of a side door, followed by the judge, who wore a long, black robe.

"All rise for the Honorable James A. Perkins."

The courtroom was noisy with chatter, and as the balding judge sat down at his bench he slammed the gavel. "Quiet! This is a court of law. Be seated and keep your mouths shut."

When the room was still, the judge continued. "This court is now in session. The defendant will rise and the charge against him will be read."

Murphy looked at Oberling, thinking the man should get up now and stop the trial. The lawyer gave him a blank stare.

Anger surged in Murphy and it was with great reluctance that he rose to his feet. "Your Honor, my—"

"Quiet!" The judge pointed his finger. "You will remain mute until the charges have been read, and then you will be seated."

Murphy didn't listen to the bailiff's reading. His thoughts were on the night he had ridden from Vera Cruz toward Tucson with Dodson. Twice he'd had good opportunities to escape: once when the buzz of a rattlesnake had frightened Dodson's buckskin and a second time when the marshal had stopped to relieve himself.

That night had been black with no moon, and Murphy was on the dun. He wished now he had spurred the horse into a dead run, leaving Dodson far behind him. He could have headed for Nogales and easily made it across the Mexican border before anyone could stop him. Or gone back to New Mexico where he had friends who would have returned with him and helped to clear his name.

The bailiff finished reading. Judge Perkins cleared his throat. "The prosecution will call its first witness."

A name was called, and Murphy recognized the mustached cowboy who stepped up to the witness stand as being the one who'd had the rope on the Mexican padre. After he was sworn in and seated, a well-dressed, rusty-haired man moved in front of the prosecution table.

"In your own words, will you please tell this court what transpired on the day George Anderson and Johnny Tubbs were murdered . . . uh, excuse me, your Honor, I mean killed."

"Well, sir," the cowboy glanced nervously at Murphy. "Some of us boys was ridin' into Vera Cruz to have us a beer when a Mexican pullin' a donkey and cart run out in front of us in the street. It caused a heck of a wreck. When it was over with, George and Johnny went to cussin' the Mexican for what he'd done, and that fellow there"—he gestured at Murphy—"why he come up out of nowhere and went to sidin' with the Mexican.

"Pretty soon he just got mad and opened up with his flamethrower and shot 'em both down. They wasn't wearin' no guns. None of us were, 'cept one or two of us had a rifle in our saddle scabbards."

"You are absolutely certain George and Johnny were weaponless?"

"Of course I am. I was there, wasn't I?"

"And did George or Johnny threaten to strike anyone? Did their quarrel with the defendant or the Mexican go beyond just words?"

"No, sir. They didn't do anything."

"Do you remember how many shots were fired?"

"Not really. Maybe three or four."

"Are you absolutely sure the defendant, this man here"—the attorney moved within a few feet of Murphy and gestured at him—"was the man you saw shoot down George Anderson and Johnny Tubbs in cold blood?"

"It was him, all right."

"And what did the defendant do after the shooting?"

"Why he just walked away like none of it mattered one bit. A few days later I heard he was the new marshal in Vera Cruz, and I wondered about it but there wasn't much I could do."

"Thank you very much." The lawyer turned to Oberling. "Your witness."

Oberling stood facing the judge. "The defense has no questions at this time."

The judge excused the witness, and four others were called, each reciting the same story. Murphy was fuming. Oberling hadn't done a thing to dispute any of the testimony, although Murphy had thoroughly briefed him on every detail of the events that had occurred the day of the shooting.

All at once Murphy realized what a fool he had been. Oberling had to be a plant, appointed by the judge and hired by King to make sure no other defense attorney became involved. Ben King had done his homework. The plot was working well, so well, in fact, that Murphy couldn't see a hole in it big enough for a mouse to climb through.

"Defense counsel," the judge said, "the prosecution has rested for the moment and you are now free to call your witnesses."

"Your Honor"—Oberling stood—"I'm afraid my defense is sadly lacking and I apologize to the court for my unpreparedness. Although my client proclaims his innocence, I have not been able to find, nor has he been able to provide, a single witness to substantiate his plea of not guilty. I—"

Murphy jumped to his feet, unable to hold back his rage. "Your Honor, he is a liar! I have witnesses and I request a continuance of this trial to give me time to find new counsel and get them here."

The judge slammed his gavel. Deputies Copeland and Posey grabbed Murphy and shoved him back into his chair.

"This is my courtroom," the red-faced judge sputtered. "I will decide who will be allowed to speak and when. There will be no continuance and I see no reason to believe your word over Mr. Oberling's. One more outburst from you and I'll have you removed from these proceedings and charged with contempt."

He looked at Oberling, and the volume of his voice lowered. "You may continue your discourse, counsel."

"That is all I have to say, Your Honor. The defense rests with no argument or charge to the jury."

"Very well. If no further witnesses are to be called, the prosecution may make its closing remarks."

Murphy quit listening. He nodded his head down, looking at no one. In the course of duty he had been involved in murder trials that had lasted over a month. This one would be over by noon on the first day. His attorney, the judge, the witnesses, and likely the jury were set to convict him before he ever walked in the room. He had no chance at justice—or freedom.

Like never before, Murphy understood why many people he'd met despised the courts and the men who served them. They had either been victims of power and abuse within the legal system or knew of someone who had.

If his sentence was delayed long enough and he was

somehow able to get another attorney and file an appeal, and if a higher court was to eventually set him free, he resolved to never forget this day. Men like Oberling and the judge were worse than hardened criminals who made no pretext about who they were or what they had done. And they deserved harsher punishment.

The prosecution finished and the judge turned his attention to the twelve-member jury. "Gentlemen, the accused is charged with first-degree murder. You have heard the testimony and the facts relating to this case, and it is now your job to render the defendant and this court a verdict of guilty or not-guilty. If you find the defendant guilty as charged, you have decided that the killing of George E. Anderson and Johnny K. Tubbs was unlawful and that it was deliberate and premeditated.

"To reach a guilty verdict of second-degree murder, you have decided the unlawful killing was with malice aforethought but without deliberation and premeditation. In other words the accused intended to hurt the victims, but he did not intend to kill them. To reach a guilty verdict of manslaughter you have determined the unlawful killing was without malice aforethought and that the defendant killed the victims in a state of rage, terror, or desperation."

The judge stood. "The jury will retire for deliberations." He slammed his gavel. "This court is adjourned until further notice."

Deputy Copeland took hold of Murphy's collar roughly. "Time to go. Pick up your ball."

Murphy hadn't been back in his prison room for much over a half hour when Copeland opened the door. "Jury's back in. Get movin'."

Earl Posey rose from his chair across from Murphy. "Cain't we take the leg chain off him? He ain't goin' nowhere with both of us a-watchin' him and he cain't hardly get up and down them stairs with it on."

"Nope. Dodson wants it left on, and if I had my way we'd

chain the other leg and put a collar around his neck too. Come on. We got to hurry. The judge is waiting."

As Murphy entered the courtroom and was led to his chair beside Oberling, his eyes met Ben King's. The man was grinning broadly.

The judge hammered down his gavel. "This court is now in session." He turned in his chair. "Has the jury reached a verdict?"

A middle-height, blocky man with a scrubbed stubborn look about him rose. "We have, Your Honor."

"And what is that verdict?"

"We find the accused guilty as charged."

The courtroom grew noisy. The decision was what Murphy knew it would be and he showed no emotion.

"Quiet!" The judge waited until the room was still. "At this time I would like to thank the jury for their deliberations and their speedy response to the cause of justice."

He shifted to face Murphy. "The defendant will rise."

Murphy stood.

"Normally," the judge continued, "I delay sentencing until I have had time to reflect and consider any mitigating circumstances. However this cause is clear-cut and the law prescribing the punishment for first-degree murder is well defined.

"Therefore, three days from now, on Monday morning at eleven o'clock, this court sentences you to be executed. You will be hanged by the neck until dead. May God have mercy on your soul."

CHAPTER 9

MURPHY LOOKED OUT the window at the new day, which promised to be his last. Dark circles surrounded his red, bloodshot eyes, and his brain was numb from having gone three nights with hardly any sleep.

The dying part wasn't what bothered him so much. He had no family and he'd already lived longer than a lot of men. Sooner or later death came to everyone, and the fact that he was to go with his neck in a degrading hangman's noose made little difference.

But the idea of Ben King, Dodson, and the others getting away with their bloodthirsty schemes was something he couldn't get used to. These men had to be stopped, and if for no other reason, Murphy needed to live—wanted to live. Yet escape was virtually impossible, and his feeling of complete helplessness was tearing him apart.

Deputy Earl Posey shifted his weight and his chair creaked loudly. "Yer breakfast is gettin' cold and if you won't eat it, at least drink your coffee."

Murphy turned around and took the cup off the small table between them. "What time is it?"

Posey pulled out his pocket watch. "Nearly seven."

Four hours. That's all I have left. Murphy took a swallow and set the cup down. "I need to go to the privy, Earl."·

"All right. I'll send the runner along for Copeland or one of the other deputies."

Since the trial, Dodson had ordered the center eyebolt floor chain to be locked to Murphy's handcuffs at all times with the exception of when he needed to relieve himself. Then, a minimum of two deputies had to be there to remove the chain and both of them had to accompany Murphy to and from the outhouse.

Presently Copeland walked in, holding the key. "Well, don't you look fine. How does it feel to be about to get your neck stretched? Hey, I got me a new Colt." He drew the shiny gun and pointed it at Murphy's head. "Want to see how it shoots?"

"Cut it out, Cope," Earl said. "Unlock him. He's been waitin' long enough."

The trip to the privy was more an excuse for Murphy to get out of the room and move around than it was a need. When he stepped out of the building into the sun, a slight breeze penetrated the stubble of beard on his face and he wanted to stop and relish the fresh, invigorating touch of it.

To the side, not far from the outhouse, a Mexican boy was sitting on the ground, playing in the dirt. The boy raised his head to look at them and Murphy's heart leaped.

Gabriel.

Copeland shoved Murphy on, and Gabriel busily returned to his dirt pile. Inside the privy, Murphy set the iron ball on the plank floor and excitedly inspected the dim interior. Gabriel hadn't traveled clear to Tucson to sit behind the courthouse and play in the dirt like a child. He was up to something.

The catalog on the seat bench used for toilet paper was where it always was, but a couple more old catalogs had been haphazardly stuffed in a corner. Quickly Murphy removed the top one and ruffled through the pages of the next. His fingers touched steel.

The gun was a Remington pocket revolver chambered for five rounds of .30 short rim-fire cartridges. Murphy pulled the hammer back and rotated the cylinder to check the loads, wondering where Gabriel had gotten the weapon.

He reached down and picked up the iron ball, holding

it between his hands. He wanted to rush out the door shooting, and it took all the sense his tired mind could muster to keep from doing just that. Five shots was all he had, five chances at freedom, and he must use them wisely.

"Hurry up in there," Copeland shouted.

Murphy cocked the hammer and held the gun ready. He had no use for Copeland, yet he didn't want to have to kill him if there was any way he could get around it.

A minute later the door swung open. "What the—"

Murphy fired.

The bullet struck Copeland's left collarbone and he pitched backward.

Earl Posey was going for his sidearm.

"Don't Earl!" Murphy called, stepping outside. "Don't. I don't want to shoot you."

Posey's gun was in his hand and coming up. Bewilderment mixed with fear twisted his face, and his eyes were bugged out wide.

Murphy could wait no longer. He fired, knocking one of Posey's legs out from under him. The deputy fell and Murphy hurried to him, almost tripping over his leg chain.

Earl's gun was still in his hand and Murphy stepped on the deputy's wrist, laid the Remington down, and wrenched the weapon from his hand.

Shouts came from the direction of the courthouse. Murphy quickly stuffed the Remington in his pants pocket and rose with Posey's long-barreled army-issue Colt. Two men were coming off the courthouse porch steps and he fired a round, kicking up dust in front of them.

"Señor Murphy! Señor Murphy!" Gabriel was rounding the end of the courthouse and he was leading the dun.

Murphy started to run. The ankle chain slapped against his leg with each stride, and the movement threatened to jerk the heavy iron ball from his grasp. He bent down, holding the ball as low as he could to allow more slack and forced himself faster.

Gabriel met him. Murphy managed to get his left foot in the saddle stirrup and swing up. The leg chain was too short for the move and with his hands full he was unable to grab the saddle horn. He had started to teeter backward when Gabriel pushed him, giving him enough momentum and balance to settle into the seat.

He shoved the revolver in his waistband and grabbed the reins while cradling the iron ball precariously between his forearms. Gabriel grabbed the crook of his elbow, easily swinging his lithe body on behind.

"*Yaah, yaah.*" Murphy dug his heels into the horse's sides. The dun leaped into a gallop as a shot sounded from somewhere behind. Another gun boomed and Murphy heard a bullet whine past his ear.

"Duck, Gabriel," Murphy yelled. "Stay low."

They raced through the center of town and the farther they went, the angrier Murphy became with himself for allowing the boy to be subjected to so much danger. He shouldn't have let him get mounted, but what choice did he have?

There wasn't a second to spare, and several people had seen Gabriel leading the dun. With information from Posey and Dodson, Ben King would quickly figure out the boy had planted a gun in the privy. Gabriel was a criminal now, and Murphy was afraid his tender age wouldn't help him any more than it had Antonio and Froylan.

Reaching the outskirts of town, Murphy held the dun back a little and looked ahead at the miles and miles of empty desert. Thanks to Gabriel he was free, but for how long? Where could they go to hide or elude the posse that was sure to follow? They certainly couldn't outrun it. Though the dun was stronger and faster than most horses, he was loaded down with a saddle, two riders, and a forty-pound iron ball.

If it were only dark, Murphy thought. Dodson couldn't follow or track what he couldn't see.

Gabriel, seeming to sense Murphy's quandary, pulled on his arm and pointed at a few low hills to the east. "Go there. I know a place."

Without further deliberation Murphy turned the dun. Whatever Gabriel's idea was, it had to be better than the one he didn't have.

Minutes later Murphy looked back. A group of riders had cleared the edge of town and were following in a heated, dusty gallop. He leaned forward in the saddle and urged the dun faster.

Two miles farther the hills Gabriel had pointed to didn't look a whole lot closer than they had. The posse hadn't gained any ground, might even have lost some, and Murphy wondered how long the dun could keep up the grueling pace.

Jagged lines broke the baked earth a few hundred yards ahead and the anxiety in Murphy increased. The lines were the irregular edges of an arroyo that had been cut by centuries of flash flood water. In New Mexico he'd seen some that were as deep as seventy-five feet and at least that far or more across. The arroyos were natural barriers and many ranchers used them as a fence to control the movements of their livestock.

He wanted to pull the dun up and take the time to see if the horse could make the jump, but to do so would mean they'd lose a lot of their lead on the posse. The dun was already breathing hard, and sweat lathered his flanks and chest.

Turning and running adjacent to the arroyo until it ended or until they could find a place to cross would use up what few fast miles the horse had left in him and they'd be even farther from the hills and whatever solace was to be found there.

The ravine edge was upon them and the time for thinking was past.

"Hold on, Gabriel," Murphy hollered.

The dun gathered himself and leaped. Gabriel clutched Murphy's sides and Murphy laid his head by the horse's neck. The arroyo wasn't as wide as some, but it was plenty wide enough, and it was questionable whether the dun would make it across, considering the horse's heavy load.

Murphy could see the jagged rocks and boulders far below. If they didn't make it, death was guaranteed.

The impact of the dun's front hooves hitting solid ground was bone-jarring hard, and it was all Murphy could do to stay in the saddle while holding on to the iron ball. The edge of the ravine caved in under the weight of the horse's rear feet, and the animal slid to his front knees, carried forward only by the sheer momentum of his leap.

Dust boiled in a thick cloud. The dun scrambled wildly to get his legs under him, nearly made it, started to fall, then rose again and lunged into a run.

Murphy raised himself up, let out his breath, and leaned back in the saddle. His sides hurt from Gabriel's tenacious, flesh-tearing grip on them, and it was a few seconds before he felt the boy's fingers begin to relax. They had made it, barely.

He glanced over his shoulder, wondering what effect the arroyo was going to have on Dodson and the posse. It was one thing to chance death when you had to and another to chance it when you didn't.

The dun's breathing grew increasingly harsh, and soon Murphy reined him into a slow canter to let him blow.

Gabriel tapped his back. "Look. They will not jump. They are not brave like us."

Brave. For a moment the rigid lines in Murphy's worried expression relaxed and he halted the dun. *Desperate and scared stiff* were more the words he'd have used.

A gun boomed, and a bullet puffed the ground far behind them. The posse was stopped by the arroyo, and the impossible distance shot told Murphy they were plenty mad. He watched as they put their horses into a gallop, moving alongside the ravine edge.

"Where are we going, Gabriel?" Murphy asked, nudging the dun into a trot.

"There is a mine that goes into the mountain and comes out on the other side if you go the right way. When I was at the mission, one of the padres took me there with him many times. He liked for me to help him look for shiny rocks. I think he wanted for me to find him some silver or gold."

Murphy wasn't sure he liked the idea of giving up the dun. "Can a horse get through?"

"I think maybe. We put a donkey into there, but he did not like it very much. I had to pull on him very hard to make him go."

Murphy looked back at the posse. Someone in the group, if not Dodson himself, was sure to have traveled this direction before and would know where there was a decent place to cross the arroyo and how long it would take to get to it.

For now, the best he and Gabriel could do was gain all the lead they could; heading for the mine was as good a plan as any. If they were somehow able to avoid capture until nightfall, Murphy had a few ideas of his own.

CHAPTER 10

THE DUN SNORTED in fright. Murphy let him back up a step from the narrow, dark opening of the mine tunnel, then continued to try to gently coax him in. After several tries the horse finally walked into the musky-smelling blackness.

"Be careful, Gabriel," Murphy called, looking ahead at the faint glow of the creosote soaked board they had splintered and fashioned into a crude torch. Thanks to Earl Posey, Murphy had been able to keep his smoking tobacco, and he'd had a match to light the fire.

"I am here," the boy's voice echoed. "Are you coming?"

"Yeah. Trying to."

The dun's hooves striking the ground and mine-car rail timbers was loud in the confines of the rock walls. At one time, years ago, someone had gone to a lot of trouble and expense to dynamite a hole through this mountain, and it seemed odd that such a large project had been abandoned. Yet Murphy knew of many others similar to it.

A vein was struck and followed until it was gone and could not be located again, then it was over. Somewhere else another strike would be found, and the backbreaking work of the miners would begin all over again.

Murphy carefully tested each of his steps. The light ahead disappeared.

"Gabriel?"

The light was there again. "You should walk faster. You are very slow you know."

"Slow," Murphy muttered. "I'm handcuffed, carrying an iron ball chained to my leg. I'm leading a worn-out horse and can't see a thing and you think I'm slow?"

"I did not hear you," Gabriel called. "You want for me to come closer?"

"No. That'd make too much sense. Just stay there."

When Murphy reached Gabriel, the boy pointed at a side tunnel to the right. "This is the way. I remember very good, don't I?"

"Hope so."

Gabriel was obviously enjoying his exploration activities and he left in a hurried walk, leaving Murphy to fend for himself again in the darkness. He hadn't gone far when the movement of the torch light stopped.

"The mine. It is all closed up. I remember very good and we are going the right way. I know we are."

Murphy made it to the boy and looked at the pile of earth and rocks completely blocking the tunnel. There had been a cave-in and from the looks of it, digging through might take days, even weeks, if it could be done at all.

"Well," Murphy said, suddenly feeling awfully tired. His sleepless nights in the courthouse plus the strain and stress of their escape had worn him to a frazzle. "I guess if this is the only way out of here this ends it."

"It is the right way. I know it. I did not want to tell you because I wanted you to think I remembered, but before, a long time ago, I put a mark on a rock. The mark is still there. I found it."

Disappointed, Murphy turned the dun around, finding there was barely enough room between the tunnel walls to do so. "Go on ahead, Gabriel, but stay closer to me so I can see. That posse will be coming and we've got to get moving. Go out the same way you came in."

Gabriel started off. Murphy took a few steps and stopped. A thought struck him, and he was trying to force his weary mind to sort out the details.

"What is wrong, señor? Why is it you do not follow?"

After a long moment Murphy spoke. "I want you to take your shirt off, Gabriel. Come back here and roll it up and use the end of it to dust out every horse track or foot print that shows us turning back. It'll be a big job. You've got to erase every track we make going out, leaving only the ones we made coming in. I want Dodson to think we went through the tunnel and caused the cave-in so he couldn't follow us."

"I see," Gabriel exclaimed. "You are very smart to think of this. You want for the posse to dig and dig and to go where they think we are and we are not there. We are somewhere else."

"Yeah, that's what I want. It probably won't work, but it's worth a try. We've got to hurry and hope they don't catch us before we're out and gone."

He started walking.

"But Señor Murphy. You do not have the torch. You cannot see where you are going."

"I didn't have it coming in either. Work hard and go as fast as you can."

Outside, Murphy sat against a rock with the sun on his back, waiting on Gabriel. He raised his hands and examined the raw flesh on his wrists where the tightly fitted handcuffs had rubbed, then inspected the bruised, torn skin around the shackle on his ankle.

He put his leg down and scanned the desert for a cloud of dust that would tell him the posse was approaching. The land lay still, and he guessed the posse must have had to go a considerable distance to find a place to cross the arroyo.

Murphy's eyelids grew heavy and he fought to keep them open. He reached in his shirt pocket and took out his Durham sack, wishing he had a cup of coffee or drink of water to go with his smoke. A cigarette and a cotton-dry mouth didn't fit well together.

The cigarette was almost burned to his fingertips when Gabriel appeared.

"It is done, señor. I did a very good job. I think after we get away you will owe me a lot of money."

"You're right, Gabriel. I owe you everything I own and

then some. Now I want you to put out the torch, bury it, and follow me along dusting out every track we make."

After some difficulty and with Gabriel's help, Murphy mounted the dun. He put the horse in a slow walk, choosing a route due south. When they had passed the hills and nothing lay ahead except flat, barren desert, Murphy halted the dun and waited for Gabriel to catch up.

The boy was walking backward busily dusting out his own tracks as well as those of the dun. Murphy didn't believe the work would fool an experienced tracker for long, but the furious posse might be so anxious to get at him in the mine that they wouldn't spot the dusted trail for a while, and time was what he needed the most right now.

Gabriel drew closer and Murphy called to him. "That's enough. Shake out your shirt and climb on. We better get moving."

Sometime later they reached a well-traveled road that Murphy guessed to be the main freight trail between El Paso and Tucson. The road meant travelers he didn't want to see, yet it also meant deep, powdery dust and enough tracks to make the dun's indistinguishable among them. He pondered it briefly, put the dun in the wheel ruts heading east for a couple of hundred yards, then turned the horse around and started west.

"What are you going to do, señor?" Gabriel asked. "You are going back to Tucson. I think you are loco if you go to there."

Murphy squinted his eyes against the afternoon sun. At least three hours or more of daylight remained. "Let's hope Marshal Dodson thinks like you do. Keep watching behind and tell me if you see anyone. I'm hoping we won't have to go far before we find a place to turn off."

A few miles later the road dipped into a shallow gully and Murphy turned the dun into it and stopped. "If you will, Gabriel, get off and dust out our tracks again. This should be the last time you'll have to do it."

The boy jumped down and started unbuttoning his shirt. "I will do it. Where are we going?"

"Not far. Just a little ways up the wash."

Eventually the gully became deeper, deep enough to hide the dun, and when it made a narrow turn, Murphy swung out of the saddle, nearly falling from the weight of the iron ball in his hands. He set the ball on the ground, tied the weary dun to a mesquite root sticking out of the bank, and unsaddled the horse.

Presently Gabriel emerged. "I am done. I think you are very lucky to have me here with you."

"Couldn't make it any other way." Murphy took his hat off, lay down, and closed his bloodshot, burning eyes. He was exhausted. "Watch the dun, Gabriel. Watch his ears. He'll let you know if anyone is around. When it's dark, wake me up."

"What are you going to do in the dark?"

"Oh, there's a couple of things. Then we'll head for San Patricio." Murphy yawned, half-mumbling. "Where'd you get the gun? How'd you manage to get to Tucson?"

"Some very nice people in a wagon took me there. And then I saw this man and I remembered he owed me a lot of money. He gave me his gun, but I think it is not enough."

"You stole it, didn't you?"

"I did not steal it."

"Yes, you did."

"No, I did not!"

Murphy smiled. His voice was barely audible. "Thanks, Gabriel. Thanks for everything."

CHAPTER 11

THE NIGHT WAS pitch black, and less than a quarter of a mile away the lights of Tucson shone brightly. Murphy pulled the dun up. There had been no sign of the posse, and the few hours of sleep in the gully had strengthened him.

He cocked his elbow out for Gabriel. "Swing down. I guess we're close enough."

On the ground, Murphy dropped the iron ball to rest his arms a moment. He'd come to loathe the heavy weight, and his thoughts since waking had been focused on how he could get rid of it.

He looked up at the stars. While imprisoned in the courthouse and unable to sleep, he'd spent many hours studying the sky through the window.

"Gabriel," he said quietly. "Around midnight a quarter-moon will rise. If I'm not back here by the time you can see it clearly, I want you to ride to San Patricio. The dun's give out but with just you, he'll make it.

"Go to Risa Villabisencio's house and tell her everything that has happened. Then stay there with her."

"I will not leave."

"You have to. If I don't come back they've either got me or I'm dead, and either way you can't do a thing about it."

"You should not go to town. Somebody there will see you."

"Maybe, but because we're here so soon after leaving, I think it's the last place Dodson and his men will look. I need to get these chains off, and we need a fresh horse, some food and water. After that, if he hasn't left yet, there's a lawyer I sure would like to have a visit with."

Murphy checked to be sure Earl Posey's Colt was tightly fitted in his waistband and that the Remington was still in his pocket. He picked up the ball, took a few steps, and turned back. "You'll go, won't you?"

"No."

"Your head's harder than mine, Gabriel. Guess I'll just have to make sure I make it back so we can ride to Risa's together. You'll like her. She makes the best menudo and tortillas you'll ever eat."

Murphy edged along the side of the adobe-walled livery and blacksmith shop. The building was long and rectangular, with a small, windowless room in one corner; the rest of it had an open front covered by a sloping shed roof. A corral was at the far end.

There were probably one or two other liveries in town, but Murphy remembered the location of this one because he and Marshal Dodson had stabled their horses there after riding into town from Vera Cruz weeks ago.

So far, he hadn't had any trouble. By carefully choosing a route that avoided people or lighted places, he'd slipped into town unnoticed. He crept to the corner and peeked around it. Light was coming from underneath the door. Hopefully it meant the blacksmith was inside.

A horse approached in the street. Murphy plastered himself against the wall until the rider had passed, then took another look. The street was empty. From blocks down he could hear the shouts, singing, and music of a busy dance hall.

He shifted the weight of the iron ball from both hands to only his left, pulled the Colt, and stepped around the corner, knocking lightly on the door with the end of the barrel. Boards creaked inside and a stocky man with long, heavy arms and a coarse face opened the door.

Murphy shoved the revolver deep in his stomach and pulled the hammer back. "I'll kill you if I have to. Don't do anything foolish. Now back up real slow."

The blacksmith obeyed with wide eyes and Murphy closed the door with his boot heel.

"I know you," the blacksmith said in a trembling voice. "You're the feller they was goin' to hang."

"That's me. I've got nothing to lose, and killing you won't make any difference one way or another."

Murphy tried to make his voice sound as cold as he could. The truth was he'd have to be awfully hard-pressed to shoot the man and he was running a bluff. He continued. "The only chance you've got to keep on living is to break these chains off me as quickly as you can."

"Well, ah . . . but my tools. My anvil. They're outside. I have to have them."

Murphy stepped to the side. "Go on out. I'll follow. Remember, I can't miss at this range."

The blacksmith started for a lamp hanging on the wall beside his cot.

"No," Murphy said. "No light."

"But . . ."

"You can do it without it."

The night under the shed roof was void of even starlight. Murphy wasn't sure the blacksmith could do the job without a lamp, yet there was no alternative. He couldn't chance being seen, and the anvil would be too heavy to carry inside.

After using his hands to search a bench in the corner, the blacksmith moved along the back wall a few steps, stopped, and kneeled.

"Give me your leg."

Carefully keeping the Colt on the man, Murphy set the iron ball down, then apprehensively lifted his shackled foot. If he stood on one leg it would be easy for the blacksmith to grab him and throw him off balance.

"Don't make a mistake." Murphy's voice was barely above a whisper. "I promise you you'll never make another."

The iron ankle bracelet rested on something solid, which Murphy guessed to be the edge of the anvil.

"Hold it there," the blacksmith said.

A piercing ring sounded with each swing of the smith's hammer. Several blows later the bracelet broke free and Murphy put both his feet under him. It felt good to be free from the chain and ball. Awfully good.

Murphy knelt. "Now the handcuffs. Break the chain in the middle first, then work on each wrist."

The blacksmith had broken the last cuff when a man spoke from the street. "That you, Charley?"

Murphy put the muzzle of the Colt against the side of the blacksmith's head. "Yeah . . . yeah, it's me. Just finishin' up a little job."

The vague figure in the street stepped closer. "You need a lamp to see by, don't you?"

"No. I'm through."

"Well the wife's cook stove is cracked again. You think you'll have time to look at it in the morning?"

"Yeah. We'll . . . we'll work on it."

"All right then, Charley. See ya tomorrow."

The man walked on. The blacksmith stood and Murphy moved behind him. "Head for your office."

Inside, Murphy bolted the door. Instead of a few weeks, it seemed he'd spent his life in chains, and it was difficult getting use to the freedom to spread his arms and walk normally.

He went to a lone chair by a small, potbellied stove, sat down, and crossed his legs, resting the aimed revolver on his knee. "Take your clothes off."

"Me? But I did what you wanted. Ain't that enough? I won't tell a soul I ever even saw you."

"You've done fine and you're alive. Keep it that way and get those clothes off."

The blacksmith undressed to his long underwear.

"I noticed you've got a few horses in the corral," Murphy said. "They all yours?"

"No. Three of 'em are. Two are buggy horses, one, the chestnut, belongs to the banker, and the big black is Marshal Dodson's."

Murphy uncrossed his legs. "Dodson rides a buckskin?"

"Most of the time he does. The black is his Sunday horse. He uses him in parades and such."

"He keeps a saddle here, too?"

"Yeah. It's outside with the others. He's kind of proud of it, silver conches and all. Keeps it covered with a tarp."

Murphy stood and stepped toward a coil of rope hanging in a corner. Under it, propped up, was what appeared to be a long-barreled Sharps. Upon examination, he found the gun to be an old Remington rolling-block sporting rifle chambered for .44-90 center-fire cartridges. Next to the Sharps, the Remington was probably the most widely used buffalo gun on the plains.

"This thing shoot?" he asked.

"Don't know. Never tried it. A couple of years ago a fellow traded it in on a horse. He said it worked. I didn't have much in it so I just set it there. There's a box of shells for it on the shelf."

Murphy set the rifle down. "You know of an attorney named Oberling?"

"Sure. He's been in town a long time."

"Where's his house, his office?"

"It's one and the same. It's just across the street from the courthouse. He's got a room to the side where he sleeps. His shingle is hanging outside."

The nervous blacksmith was doing everything he could to please, and Murphy decided against his earlier intention of knocking the man out and tying him up. He'd just tie him up.

"Sit in the chair," he ordered.

Less than a half hour later the blacksmith was securely bound and gagged, and Murphy had the man's shirt, overalls, and hat on. Dodson's black horse was tied to a post in the corral, saddled with the Remington rifle loaded in the scabbard. A full canteen was wrapped around the horn, and in the saddlebags were two cans of the blacksmith's peaches.

Murphy blew out the coal oil lamp on the table. "Don't wear yourself out trying to get loose. It'll only get you dead. That fellow you talked to will be by in the morning. You'll be fine until then. Sometime, when I'm through this way again, I'll pay you for the food, clothes, rifle, and the trouble I've put you to."

A wagon and team moved by slowly and Murphy waited until it was past to step out and close the door. He was in high spirits. In his belt, which he had put on to hold the too-large overalls tighter around his waist, were the Colt and the Remington pocket pistol. His chains were off and it more than slightly amused him to steal Dodson's horse and saddle. The evening couldn't have gone any smoother, and if his luck held and Oberling hadn't left town yet, there remained but one thing left to do.

He crossed the street and walked along the building fronts, keeping to the shadows as much as possible. While he wasn't overly concerned about being seen in his disguise, he didn't want to talk to anyone.

A few blocks past the noisy dance hall he'd heard earlier, the outline of the courthouse loomed on his left. Murphy slowed his walk until finally stopping under a faded business sign barely readable in the darkness: THOMAS OBERLING, ATTORNEY AT LAW.

Light filtered around the edges of a shaded window in

the clapboard wall. Murphy moved quietly to the door and turned the knob, surprised that it was unlocked. He pulled the Colt and warily stepped inside.

"Who's there? I'll be out in a moment." The impatient sounding voice was Oberling's, and it was coming from an open doorway to the side.

Murphy gently closed the door and surveyed the room. A large, expensive-looking mahogany desk was in the center, with two matching leather-padded chairs positioned in front. Heavily tasseled and fringed draperies covered the walls, and a thick wool carpet was on the floor. Oberling had spent a good deal of money to impress his clients, and Murphy wondered how much of it was Ben King's.

He crept to the doorway and looked in. Oberling had a suitcase in one hand and was taking another one off the bed. Murphy stepped out, aiming the Colt. He pulled back the hammer, and the click of it was loud in the stillness.

"What the—"

"Good evening, Mr. Oberling," Murphy said sarcastically. "I'm so glad I caught you in."

"Who are you?"

"You mean you don't recognize me? Guess it's the chains. I must look different without them."

Oberling closed his eyes and rocked back and forth. For a moment, Murphy thought he was going to pass out.

"Put down your luggage. You're not going anywhere. If you do everything I tell you, you *might* live through this night."

The frail attorney opened his eyes and dropped his bags. "It wasn't me. I knew you weren't guilty. I wanted to defend you. But Mr. King . . . the judge, they swore they'd ruin me if I didn't do what they said. They were going to take away everything: my license, my business, my property. It has taken me thirty years to accumulate what little I have."

"Seems like a big waste of time to me." Murphy entered the bedroom to get closer. "How much did King pay you to do his dirty work?"

"Pay? He didn't pay me. He threatened me. He—"

Murphy slapped Oberling with the back of his hand. The blow wasn't meant to be hard, yet it knocked the lawyer on to the bed.

"How much?" Murphy grabbed him by the collar and pulled him up. "Tell me or I'll beat you until you do."

"A . . . a thousand dollars. But I didn't want it. He made me take it."

"Shut up!" Murphy threw Oberling back down. He picked up one of the suit cases, opened it, and dumped the contents. A quick search revealed nothing of interest, and he dumped the other one.

"Where's the money?"

"I don't have it. It's in the bank."

Murphy grabbed a handful of the lawyer's hair and jerked him headfirst into the pile of clothes on the floor. He put his boot on Oberling's neck.

"This is the last time I'm going to ask you. Tell me where the money is."

"All right. Please. Let me up. The money's here. I'll get it for you."

Murphy removed his foot, and Oberling frantically searched the pile, scattering the clothes. He came to a black coat, unfolded it, and reached into an inside pocket, bringing out a leather bag.

"Here. Take it. It's all there."

Murphy opened the bag. A thick roll of bills was inside. He guessed Oberling was lying and there might be more money hidden elsewhere in the coat or the clothes, but this was enough. He'd only given himself so much time, and Gabriel was alone in the desert anxiously waiting for him.

"On your feet, Oberling. You're going to your desk to write a letter explaining everything you, the judge, Dodson, Ben King, and the bought witnesses did to try to frame and hang me."

With occasional input from Murphy, the attorney meekly wrote out a two-page letter. Murphy was fully aware that the credibility of a forced confession would be questionable, yet the letter was better than nothing and in the right hands it might be enough to prompt a government investigation of the court.

A whistle blew in the distance, and Oberling pushed his chair back. "The train. I was planning to be on it. My sister is terribly ill and I was leaving to be with her."

"I doubt you even have a sister, but, if you do, the only reason you'd be going is because you think she'll die and you want to be there to steal her estate. You're nothing but a snake!"

With that, Murphy let the hammer down on the Colt and hit the lawyer over the head with the barrel. Oberling flopped forward on the desk, started to rise, and Murphy hit him again, harder. The man fell sideways from his chair and lay still on the carpet.

Soon Murphy had Oberling tied and gagged with strips he'd cut from a bed sheet. He pocketed the letter and money, blew out the lamp, and locked the door as he stepped outside.

A faint glow was in the east, showing the coming moon, and Murphy hurried back to the livery. There should be ample time left to meet Gabriel, yet he was worried the independent boy might take it upon himself to come looking.

Murphy found the black as he had left him. He snugged up the horse's cinch, led him out of the corral, and was about to mount when he remembered his promise to pay the blacksmith. He fished two bills out of the leather pouch and stuffed them in the corral gate latch so they would fall when the rail slid open. Then he put his foot in the stirrup and swung in the saddle.

The horse snorted and pranced sideways. Murphy could feel the pent-up energy and power in the animal caused by too much grain and too little use. Except for the gait, Pena's sorrel had felt much the same at first, but the horse had no bottom to him. By dawn Murphy knew he'd find out if Dodson's black was worth as much as the man apparently thought he was.

Later, after leaving town by the same route he had taken going in, Murphy let the eager horse move into a lope. The tip of the quarter-moon was showing and although he had a general idea where he had left Gabriel, there were no landmarks or changes in the terrain to help him determine the exact location.

An odd feeling came over Murphy, an uncertainty, and it was some time before he realized what was causing it.

While in confinement in the courthouse jail, nothing had really changed. Except for being framed and charged for a crime he didn't commit, Al Murphy was the same man he had always been. But today, for the first time in his life, he had crossed over the line.

Regardless of the reasons, and they were the best anyone could have, he had seriously wounded one lawman and crippled another, forced two citizens to do his bidding at gunpoint—taking money from one of them—and stolen a horse and saddle. He was an outlaw, a long-rider.

Murphy imagined what a wanted poster on him would look like and what his reaction to it would be if he'd seen it while going through posters at his office as sheriff of Turrett County, New Mexico. The poster would show the deeds of a hardened criminal, a murderer, the kind of man Murphy would have tracked down and extradited back to Arizona.

How many men, Murphy wondered, had he jailed or

killed who were no different from himself? Men who had simply been at the wrong place at the wrong time and were forced by circumstances to do things they normally would not have done. ❋

His thinking upset him, and he shook his head as if the action would erase the chalkboard in his mind. Moments later, in a sincere, analytical effort to justify his life and the day's events, he searched his motives, concluding that although his methods were sometimes questionable, the reasons behind them had been and still were upright and pure.

He believed his principles were intact, that he knew and respected the difference between right and wrong, and that somewhere within those boundaries he had fought to survive and would continue to do so.

His thoughts somewhat settled, Murphy looked around him and back at the lights of Tucson. He realized he must be fairly close to the place he had left Gabriel.

"Gabriel," he called softly. He rode on, slowly, continuing to call now and then. Finally he heard the boy answer.

"I am here."

By the time Murphy reached him, Gabriel was mounted on the dun.

"Anyone come by?" Murphy asked.

"No. I did not see no one. Where did you get the horse?"

"In town, at the livery."

"You stole the horse, didn't you?"

"Yeah, that's just what I did. One of these days me and you are going to have to stop taking other people's things. Might turn into a habit.

"Well," Murphy took off his hat and ran his hand through his hair. "Let's get to San Patricio. I could stand about two dozen bowls of Risa's menudo."

They hadn't gone far when Gabriel spoke. "I must admit something to you, señor. You know the gun? I told you a lie. I did steal it from somebody."

"I know, Gabriel. I know."

CHAPTER 12

THE MORNING SUN was bright as Murphy and Gabriel turned their horses up the path leading to the Villabisencio hacienda. There was no breeze; the air was thick, stifling, holding the promise of an unmercifully hot day.

Murphy slumped forward in the saddle and rode like a sack of potatoes, his body wearily giving to the horse's movements. Dodson hadn't misjudged the black. The horse was still fresh enough to go the night's ride over again and then some.

But Murphy was worn out. The strength he'd obtained from the few hours' sleep he'd gotten in the ravine a hundred years ago had left him; it was all he could do to hold his eyes open.

No one could be seen around the house. Murphy stopped in front of the garden and half slid to the ground. Water had pooled in a nearby irrigation ditch and he went to it, dropping to his knees and splashing the water on his face and neck.

"Al Murphy!"

Murphy looked up to see Risa rounding the corner of the house, rushing toward him. He stood and wiped his face with his shirtsleeve.

She hugged him briefly. "I was certain something had happened to you. It has been so long since you left."

"A lot has happened, Risa." Murphy gestured at the horses and the boy who was still sitting on the dun. "His name is Gabriel. He's a good friend. Saved my life. We could sure use a cup of coffee."

"Of course." She stepped to the boy. "My name is Risa.

Will you come inside and have something to eat? There is a berry pie in the oven."

He swung down and smiled. Anyone looking would never guess that he hadn't slept in thirty hours. "I am Gabriel."

After caring for the horses, Murphy and Gabriel washed in the metal washtub underneath the window in the kitchen and then sat down at the table. While they ate, Murphy told Risa everything that had happened since he'd left. She listened intently, without interruption, and although Murphy could see nothing in any of it he thought was good news, her eyes held a lively sparkle that hadn't been there the last time he'd seen her.

She filled Gabriel's tall glass with milk for the third time and poured Murphy the last cup of coffee in the pot before sitting down.

"I am sorry for the trouble you have been through. But there is hope. My husband and sons may be alive. A few days ago a vaquero riding through on his way to Mexico stopped at el señor Pena's store. He asked Pena about a large mine he had seen where there were many men with guns guarding it. He said he could only see from a distance, but he thinks the miners there were slaves—Apaches and perhaps some Mexicans."

"Where is it?"

"El señor Pena had the vaquero draw a map. The mine is hidden in a deep canyon on Ben King's rancho. El señor Pena was a soldier and an officer in the Mexican War. He is a good friend of my husband. He has been busy gathering guns, and he is gathering the men here to go there and fight."

She took a breath. "We believe the reason Santiago, Froylan, and Antonio's bodies were not found is because they are not dead. They are working with the other slaves in the mine."

For the first time since hearing about the disappearance

of Santiago and his sons, Murphy was encouraged. Still, he had reservations. King had to know about Santiago's education, his contacts in the territorial government, and his many years of service to the poor and oppressed in the area.

A man like Santiago was dangerous to King's operations. Why then, after the rancher had him, would he let him live? He wouldn't, unless he was absolutely certain Santiago was in a place from which he could not escape.

Maybe King believed the mine was such a place, Murphy concluded. The wealthy man might even derive a warped sense of pleasure out of watching Santiago carry sacks of ore on his back like a mule. Froylan and Antonio, both young and strong, would make good laborers, perhaps providing King with yet another source of amusement.

"Does Pena have any idea how many men are guarding the mine?"

"No. He only knows what the vaquero told him—that there were many."

Murphy tapped out the last of the tobacco in his Durham sack onto a cigarette paper.

"Risa"—he looked at her—"I know you want someone to go to the mine and do something, and the sooner the better. But before Pena or any of us starts rushing out there we better have some idea of what we're up against. If Santiago and your sons are there, we have to try and make sure our actions don't put their lives in any more danger than they already are."

"I will go there," Gabriel interjected. "I am very good at sneaking around and finding out things. In Vera Cruz, I know about everything."

Murphy smiled at him. "You're the best, but it's too risky. I want you to stay here with Risa." He glanced at her. "You could use some help, couldn't you?"

"Oh yes. When I am not working in the field or the garden I have been building a new chicken house."

Gabriel set his glass down. A milk mustache covered the top of his lip. "I think I will go back to Vera Cruz. There are men there who will pay me a lot of money."

Murphy remembered the leather pouch he had taken from Oberling. He licked and sealed his cigarette, letting it hang from the corner of his mouth, and removed the pouch from a large front pocket in the overalls. Opening it, he took out a roll of bills, removed two, and laid them in front of Gabriel.

"There's two hundred dollars. A hundred is for what you've already done and a hundred is for what you're going to do, which is to stay here and help Risa."

Risa's expression showed her astonishment at so much money being given to a boy, yet she remained silent. Gabriel picked up the bills and studied them, obviously trying not to let his excitement show.

"You stole the money, didn't you?"

"Yeah and we're not going to talk about it. You want the job or not?"

"I think maybe . . ."

"No maybes. It's either yes or no, and you have to promise to stay here and work until I tell you different."

"I will stay." Gabriel carefuly folded the money. "I think I might have to go to the store today and buy something."

Murphy grinned. "I expect so. Now go on outside and find some work to do."

Gabriel left and Murphy put three bills in the pouch, shoved it back in his pocket, and pushed the rest across the table to Risa. "Keep it. Use what you need to."

She let the money lay on the table. "So you are planning to go to the mine?"

He nodded, lighting his smoke. The coffee had helped to revive him and his thoughts were clear. "I'll sleep today and leave tonight. We need to know how well guarded the place is, and if I can find it out, it would help to know for sure if Santiago and the boys are there.

"In the middle of all this, I have another problem. I'm a convicted murderer and there will be a price put on my head. Half of Arizona will be hunting me within a week. The only chance I have is to get to the governor with the letter from the crooked attorney in Tucson I told you about and hope he will listen to me and launch an investigation."

Murphy took a sip of coffee. "It might be, depending on what the situation at the mine really is and how willing the governor is to help, that it would be wise to wait and let him handle it. Because Apaches are involved, he may be able to persuade the army to send troops from Fort Smith. It would only take them a few days to get here."

Risa's face was grave with doubt, but Murphy continued. "Look. I know Mister Pena means well, but the men here are farmers, not fighters. They won't stand a chance against King's seasoned riflemen. It will be a slaughter, and if I know Santiago at all, he wouldn't want that. He'd rather die himself first."

Risa put her elbows on the table and held her face in her hands. Finally she spoke. "You are right. My husband would not want a single man in this valley to die because of him."

"How far is Prescott from here?" Murphy asked.

"I am not sure. Perhaps four days in a buggy."

"Then I should make it in three. I'll go to the mine tonight and at daylight see what I can. If it looks like it's too well guarded for us to be able to do much, I'll head for Prescott and the governor."

He paused. "Today is Tuesday, isn't it?"

"Yes."

"If you haven't heard from me by next Tuesday, you can figure you won't."

Risa sighed and rose from the table. "You are tired. You must rest."

Murphy put his cigarette out. "I suppose I better. I'm a

little worried about leaving Gabriel here. Dodson could show up in the village looking for me, and if he sees Gabriel and recognizes him as the boy who was in the marshal's office in Vera Cruz, he'll make it rough on him."

"I will watch him closely. He will be safe."

"Well, I guess that's all we can do. It should take Dodson a while to figure out where I am, but if he shows up today, the horses will be a dead giveaway."

"Gabriel and I will find a place for them."

"And Risa. You might go to the store with Gabriel. I'm out of smoking tobacco and I could use a set of clothes that halfway fit and a holster and gun belt if Pena has it. I need some shells too. A box of thirty shorts and a box of Colt forty-fives."

She nodded.

Murphy stood and scratched his wrist. Risa noticed the raw flesh where the handcuff had been.

"Sit down," she said. "I will get some salve and bandages."

CHAPTER 13

THERE WAS NO sign of the coming dawn in the sky, yet instinct told Murphy it would be here soon, and that bothered him. Before leaving Risa's he had memorized the vaquero's map, and although the darkness made it difficult to identify landmarks, he felt like he should have come across the canyon holding the mine by now.

The dun he was leading whinnied, and Murphy reined the black to a halt so he could listen for the answer of a nearby horse. Presently a lone coyote howled in the distance, and hearing nothing else, Murphy nudged the black on with a pair of expensive, silver spurs Gabriel had bought him.

Because Dodson or someone else in Tucson had taken everything in his saddlebags except his badge, which had fallen into the folds of a corner and was hidden, the boy had also bought him a pair of used binoculars to replace the ones he had lost.

He hadn't had the chance to thank Gabriel. Risa, thinking he needed the rest and that it would only take a few hours of riding to get to the mine, hadn't roused him until midnight, and by that time Gabriel was sound asleep.

Murphy reached back and felt the stock of the Remington buffalo rifle, making sure it was snug in the scabbard, then he checked the buckled flaps on his saddlebags. Risa had filled them with dried meat and fruit, some fresh garden stuff, and a round tin of tortillas. He guessed the bags weighed twenty-five pounds and had enough food in them to last a month, especially considering the amount of menudo he had eaten before he left.

Risa had done an expert job of estimating his size, and the new denim clothes she had purchased fit perfectly. She'd also bought him an extra shirt, which was packed with the food, a new, gray hat, the gun belt and holster he had requested, and a box of .45s. Pena's mercantile didn't have the .30 shorts.

Murphy started to reach in his shirt pocket for his tobacco, then changed his mind. He had no idea how close he might be to the canyon, and a watchful guard stationed on a rim or point might spot the glow. He hadn't gone far when the dun whinnied again, and this time he caught the barely audible answer of a horse somewhere to his right.

He stopped and stepped down, leading the horses while hunting for a place to tie them that offered at least some concealment. He had brought the dun along in the likelihood that he would be going to Prescott and would need the strength of both horses to make the fast trip. Then too, should a posse come upon him, a fresh mount would be a mighty handy thing to have.

The eastern horizon showed a hint of gray. Murphy continued to walk until he came across a low place covered with thick, tall mesquite. While he couldn't be sure how well the thicket would hide the horses in the impending daylight, it was as good, perhaps better, than any other he might find. He tied the horses securely, removed the Remington rifle from the scabbard, and took his binoculars from the saddlebags. The horse he'd heard might just be a ranch horse turned out on the range to fend for himself, but Murphy doubted it. Odds were the horse was at the mine.

He walked, taking long, quick steps. If he could reach the edge of the canyon before it was light it would make it easier to avoid being seen.

A while later he lay on his stomach beneath two greasewoods, looking down. The sun was barely showing, and already the floor of the deep, short canyon was a blur of activity. Men, donkeys, mules, and wagons were scurrying here and there like so many ants, most of them moving toward an immense dark hole at one end. The hole was much larger than any mine entrance Murphy had ever seen, and he guessed it had to be the natural entrance to a cave of enormous proportions.

Only two buildings below were of any significance, the rest being brush-roofed sheds and lean-tos. One of them was substantially constructed of heavy railroad timbers, with a new tin roof and a corral attached to it, where several horses were standing.

The other, about four to five times larger, was a haphazard affair of adobe at the bottom, tarps, boards, pieces of tin, and a woven brush roof that was partially covered with mud.

Being careful to hold his fingers around the front binocular rings so they wouldn't glare in the sunlight, Murphy adjusted the focus to study the men. Most of them did appear to be Apaches, some wearing only a loincloth. Others were fully dressed, and on one, though it was too far and the magnification of the binoculars too weak, he thought he saw a beard. This man had to be Mexican or white because Apaches detested facial hair and would pull it out if it grew.

Murphy counted twenty-one guards carrying rifles, and on glassing the rim opposite him, saw five more. If the wall he was on held another five that made over thirty, and he wasn't sure that he had seen them all. Thirty men with repeating rifles was a formidable force. However, a company or two of army infantry could handle them, probably forcing a surrender without having to fire a shot.

Murphy scanned a ribbon of road that zigzagged up a steep canyon bank at the opposite end from the mine. Near the top the road followed the bed of a short, narrow gorge, and from what he could tell, this was the only exit or entrance to the box canyon. While a group of armed men stationed there could easily keep anyone from coming in, another group located at the top could just as easily stop anyone from leaving.

He looked back in the bottom. Directly beneath him he was surprised to see something he had missed. Several Indian women and children were standing in a line, unloading firewood from a wagon. Although the ledge prevented him from seeing the end of the human chain, he assumed that the wood was for cooking fires positioned against the canyon wall to filter the smoke.

The whole operation was astonishing, and Murphy marveled at how an operation as big as this could be kept secret for so long. Yet he could see how it was possible. Unless a rider, such as the drifting vaquero, accidentally wandered right to it, the mine was extremely well hidden by seemingly endless miles of flat, desert terrain.

And who was likely to venture out here? There were no valleys, hills, stream beds, or rocky outcrops to draw a miner's interest. The bunch grass was too scarce to support a sheep or a goat herder. That left an occasional cowboy hunting what few cows that could survive on this barren section of wasteland, and since it was King's range, he would be working for the rancher.

Murphy scooted back from the edge on his elbows. He had futilely tried to determine if Santiago was among the hundred or more slaves below. The distance was too great, and after all these years the small man's looks would probably have changed. He didn't think he would recognize Antonio or Froylan if they were standing right in front of him.

Nonetheless, he was fairly sure that some of the men were of Mexican descent, and that gave him hope.

He squirmed around on his stomach to look in the direction where he had left the horses. The land lay flat, with only an occasional greasewood or mesquite for cover. He had known his return trip would be more difficult to make without being seen, but now, in the full daylight, it appeared impossible.

There was no other alternative. To stay where he was and wait for nightfall would waste a full day of riding and increase the odds that someone would find him or the horses.

Several yards to his left was a shallow wash, barely more than the width of his body deep, and he wormed toward it, holding the rifle in front of him with both hands. His muscles were tense, so tense they trembled.

One foot at a time. Over and over the words went through his mind not allowing other thoughts to enter. He paused beneath a mesquite bush and wiped the stinging sweat out of his eyes. The wash had become a little deeper and he had gone a fair stretch.

He looked behind him through the branches of the bush and his heart stopped. A man with a rifle was slowly walking along the canyon rim, nearing the spot where he had been. By moving over the ground like a snake Murphy had avoided being seen, but he had left a trail that would be hard for anyone to miss.

The guard turned and stood with his back to Murphy, looking down at the mine. Murphy crouched low and, stepping as lightly as he could, hurried on, half-expecting to hear the sharp report of a gun and feel the impact of a bullet. Whether the guard eventually noticed the trail or not, his best bet was to get to the horses as quickly as he could.

Although the landscape appeared to hold no place where an animal the size of a horse could be hidden, Murphy was almost upon the black and the dun before he spotted them. He untied them, shoved the Remington in the scabbard, and mounted, leaving the binoculars hanging from his neck.

He rode at a walk, not wanting to kick up any dust. With his naked eye he couldn't see a soul. Perhaps, if he was lucky, no one could see him.

CHAPTER 14

AL MURPHY STEPPED into a small, dirt-floored cantina located on the outskirts of Prescott. It was midmorning and there were no other customers. He sat down at a table in the corner, took off his hat, and beat it against his leg to shake loose the trail dust.

He had made the trip from the mine on King's ranch in seventy-two hours, stopping only twice to sleep. To avoid being seen, he'd stayed away from the roads and that had cost him some time.

A handsome woman, perhaps in her late forties, with black hair generously sprinkled with gray, appeared through a side door and moved toward him. "Yes, señor. What may I get for you?"

"I'd like a shot of tequila, ma'am, and a tall glass of beer to go with it."

She started for the bar and what few bottles were on a shelf behind it.

"Ah, ma'am. Maybe you'd better bring the bottle."

Murphy's first drink burned his dry throat. The second went down easier, and by the third he was beginning to feel the alcohol's calming effects. He relished the feeling, pouring himself another shot.

Since coming to Arizona his life had been a turbulent whirlwind of worry, fights, hard riding, and precious little rest. And what had been accomplished? Two men were dead, he was a convicted murderer, and Santiago and his sons were still missing.

He tossed down the shot and sipped his beer. Presently his thoughts drifted to a gentler time in his life.

There was a small log cabin in a meadow of green, knee-high grass. The place wasn't much, but it was a start, the beginning of the Wyoming horse ranch he had always dreamed about.

The scene changed. His wife Midge was sitting inside the cabin on the bed, brushing her long brown hair in the flickering light of the rock fireplace. She was a beautiful woman, a good woman, better than any man could ask for and much better than he deserved.

Murphy tried in vain to hold the picture, to not let it change like it always did.

Midge was lying on the ground. Her head was in his lap, her face soiled and bruised, her blue eyes open.

She was dead.

He blamed himself. He shouldn't have gone into town after supplies, shouldn't have left her alone.

A few months later, after he had tracked down and killed the seven horse thieves who had chased her, who had caused her horse to stumble and fall thereby breaking her neck, he had drifted. For years he traveled to nowhere in particular, drinking up what money he happened to come across. Life held no meaning, and he didn't care whether he lived or died.

Until he happened upon a murder outside of Turrett, New Mexico, and through a series of events became involved in a struggle between two rival mercantile businesses. The local sheriff died in the conflict and at the town's insistance Murphy once again pinned on the badge. The new job and a handful of friends had given him a new lease on life.

"Señor."

The voice broke Murphy's thoughts and he looked up at the woman. "Yes."

"Is there something else I can get for you?"

"No, ah, gracias." He shoved the bottle farther away, stood up, and finished the last swallow of his beer. "I've had too much already. What do I owe you?"

He paid the bill, leaving a large tip, and walked outside. Although his saddlebags were full of food, he hadn't eaten since yesterday evening and on an empty stomach the tequila was hitting him hard.

He moved to the dun, untied him, and checked the latigo. Afraid that someone in Prescott might recognize Dodson's black horse, he had left him tied in a draw a mile or so outside of town.

Murphy mounted and nudged the weary horse into the street. He should have asked the woman in the cantina where the governor's mansion was. He shrugged. It shouldn't be too difficult to find.

Ten minutes later he stepped into an impressive red-brick building. A few well-dressed people were gathered in the foyer, and they stopped talking to look at him. He knew he must be a sight, unshaven and covered with trail dust.

"Any of you folks know where the governor's office is?"

For a moment it didn't look like he was going to get an answer. Finally a young fellow standing to the side beside a large painting of Ulysses Grant pointed at the stairwell. "Third story, fourth door on your right."

At the top of the stairs a tall, thin-shouldered man with a drooping gray mustache stopped him. "Sorry, mister. No firearms are allowed up here."

Murphy had half-expected as much, and although he didn't think there would be any problems he had put the small Remington pistol in his rear pocket just in case. He unbuckled his gun belt and handed it to the man, who then hung it on a wall peg.

"It'll be here when you're ready to leave."

The door to the governor's office was open and Murphy

stepped inside. He had never been to see a governor, or legislator either, and had no idea what to expect. A slight, young, clean-shaven man sitting behind a desk spoke.

"May I help you?"

"Ah, yeah. I know I look a little rough for a visit, but this is an emergency. I need to speak to the governor."

"I'm afraid that will be impossible. He won't be returning from California until sometime next week."

"That won't do," Murphy's voice was gruff and sharp. "You don't understand. I *have* to see him."

The man shrugged. "The governor's secretary is in. Perhaps I can persuade him to see you. What is your name and the nature of your business?"

He hesitated on giving out his real name, then decided it didn't matter. If he was going to get his name cleared, these people were going to have to know what it was.

"Al Murphy. I'm here because there are Apaches and Mexicans in the territory who are being forced to work as slaves."

In a few minutes the man returned from a narrow hall leading off to the side. "Step this way please."

Murphy followed him to the end of the hall, where a medium-height, almost feminine-looking man was waiting with folded arms. His hair was coal black, and he wore a brown broadcloth suit, the trousers tucked into hand-tooled boots. Murphy instinctively disliked him, yet he forced himself to be cordial. This man might well be his and Santiago's only hope.

"Mr. Murphy?"

Murphy shook hands, finding the man's weak, limp grip a perfect match to his looks.

"I'm Gene Williams. Will you step inside?"

Williams's office made Thomas Oberling's look crude: the carpet, walls, everything was white, except for the furniture, which was a dark walnut. Murphy stood just inside the door. After Williams was seated behind his desk he closed it.

"Have a seat," Williams gestured to a chair. "What is this business about slavery in the territory?"

Murphy sat down, careful to not let his spurs touch the chair legs. "Well, sir, since everything depends on you, I might as well start from the beginning. I'm the sheriff of Turrett County, New Mexico. The reason I'm here in Arizona is that a good friend of mine, Santiago Villabiscencio, and his two sons are missing. Do you know him?"

Williams shook his head. "I don't think so. However the name does seem faintly familiar."

"Well, his wife wrote me a letter asking for my help."

Murphy continued to tell his story. He had no more than finished recounting the details of his arrest, trial, and escape when Williams nervously rose from his chair.

"I know you have more to tell me and I do hate to interrupt you, but there are others who must hear you. Please, if you will wait in the reception area, I will try and get them here as promptly as possible."

He hurriedly opened the door and waited for Murphy to exit. When they reached the front desk Williams spoke to the man Murphy had talked to earlier. "See that this gentleman waits here in comfort. Bring him whatever he would like to drink."

Murphy had just started on his second cup of coffee when Williams returned. Two lawmen were with him, and they had their guns pulled and trained on him before he had any opportunity to react. The shorter of the two, a nervous little man with a long, hard-boned face, stepped closer.

"Take it easy, mister. Now stand up real slow."

"What is this?" Murphy asked, looking at Williams. He already knew what it was, knew he'd played the fool, that he'd been had, but he was stalling for time to collect himself.

Williams pointed his finger at him. "You, sir, are a killer, an escaped convict, and you will be treated as such."

The short lawman spoke again. "I told you to get to your feet."

Murphy rose slowly. His mind was made up. Two guns were pointed at him at close range and he had no chance, but he wasn't going back to jail, wasn't going to be chained like a dog and taken back to Tucson to be hanged. Dodson and Ben King weren't going to have the pleasure of watching it. He would die here. He would die right now.

Before he was fully erect he threw the cup of hot coffee in the lawman's face and plunged into him, fully expecting to hear the loud report of the man's revolver.

The shot came and a bullet tore through his side. His momentum carried him forward and he knocked the smaller man off his feet.

Murphy whirled, saw the second officer's pistol leveled on him. He made a wild leap to the side where Williams was standing.

The officer's gun boomed. The shot missed. Murphy reached Williams with flinging arms and managed to grab the man and take him crashing to the floor. He got his left arm locked around Williams's neck and frantically groped in his rear pocket for the Remington.

He put the muzzle of the pistol to Williams's temple and cocked the hammer. Both lawman were standing, their guns poised and ready. The slight young man who had first greeted Murphy in the office was disappearing through the doorway into the hall.

The room was quiet, still, and the stench of burnt gunpowder was strong. Murphy rose to his feet, bringing Williams up with him and keeping the Remington shoved tightly against the side of the man's head.

Adrenaline flowed in Murphy's veins, giving him

strength while blood oozed out of the hole in his side, soaking his shirt.

He, of course, hadn't planned on this twist of events, hadn't figured on living, but he delighted in it. And though he was far from being out of danger and might not make it out of the building, let alone the town, fate had allowed him to cause some trouble and as long as life was in him, he'd cause some more of it.

The two lawmen didn't make a move. Murphy stepped to the doorway, using Williams's body as a shield.

"You won't get away, you know," the officer Murphy had knocked down threatened. "Let him go. Give it up now, and I'll talk to the judge, maybe work out a deal."

"I'm sure you'll help me all you can," Murphy replied sarcastically. "Just the same, I'll either leave or die, doesn't make much difference which, and if I go down, this fellow here goes with me."

The gray, mustached man who had earlier taken Murphy's gun belt appeared in the hall, aiming a double-barreled shotgun. "That'll be far enough. Drop your slip-gun or I'll cut you in two."

Murphy edged out into the hall so his back would be protected by the wall. He increased his arm pressure around Williams's neck.

"Afraid you have it backwards, friend. If you don't let the hammers down on that scattergun and hand it to me, I'm going to kill this man and there isn't a thing you can do about it."

Williams gulped air and spoke in a hoarse, raspy voice. "Do . . . do what he says."

The man hesitated a moment, then complied reluctantly. Murphy kept the small Remington on Williams's head while taking hold of the shotgun at the grip. He cocked both hammers with his thumb, and in a swift move took a step back and shoved the end of the twin bores in Williams's back.

Other men were trailing into the hall from the top of the stairwell. Murphy, realizing how scared and cooperative Williams was, decided he could use that. He jabbed the man with the barrel. "Tell them, tell everyone to stay clear."

Williams responded instantly, holding up his hands. "Stop. All of you stay where you are. Don't do anything."

Murphy looked at the mustached man who had handed him the shotgun. "You. Clear everybody out of the building. Anyone makes a wrong move, your governor's secretary dies."

The man stood still.

"Please, Jim," Williams whined. "He has nothing to lose. He *will* kill me."

Murphy kept his position until the two lawmen in the office had left and the hall was cleared. "All right Mr. Williams," he said quietly. "Let's go."

At the end of the hall where the stairs were, Murphy noticed that the gun belt he had checked in was gone. They moved slowly down the stairs, and by the time they reached the bottom, Murphy was feeling light-headed, the pain in his side almost unbearable.

The front door was open, and Murphy could see that several men were stationed across the street with aimed rifles resting on a barricade of barrels and crates set there for the purpose. Nonetheless, he was more concerned about the blood that was dripping off his pants leg to the floor.

"Go to the door and stand there," he said to Williams. "And don't do anything stupid."

When Williams stopped, Murphy shouted as loud as he could. "Listen to me out there. All your guns and bullets won't stop this man from dying. I want a doctor in here, and I want two fresh, saddled horses brought in."

A voice answered. "You'll get neither. Send Mr. Williams out unharmed and we'll let you go. That's our final offer."

Murphy put the Remington pistol in his waistband,

shifted the shotgun to his left hand, and jerked Williams's arm behind and up his backbone with his right until it was close to breaking.

"Talk to them," Murphy said. "Tell them."

"It is my life that is at stake," Williams cried out. "Please. I beg you. I have a wife and children. Bring the doctor and the horses. Do whatever this man asks of you."

Murphy eased the pressure on Williams's arm. Moments later the same voice responded. "All right. Give us a few minutes."

"Back up and close the door," Murphy ordered. When the door latched shut he released his hold and held the pointed shotgun in both hands. "Now close the window shades."

Murphy backed his way to a chair in the corner of the room and sat down. Sweat beaded his brow and on top of the severe pain in his side, he had become nauseous. Williams finished closing the shades and turned to face him.

"Move closer," Murphy said. "Stand in front of me."

When Williams stopped, Murphy continued. "I told you the truth. I didn't want to shoot those two cowboys in Vera Cruz. They gave me no choice. Why didn't you believe me? Are Dodson and King friends of yours?"

"Of course not. I've never met them. I . . . I should have believed you. I do believe you. If you'll let me, I can help you. On my word the governor will grant you a pardon. I—"

"Shut your lying mouth," Murphy exploded. His breathing was heavy in the following silence.

Presently a knock sounded at the door.

"If you're the doc, come on in," Murphy yelled.

An older man wearing glasses and carrying a bag appeared. He started to close the door, but Murphy stopped him.

"Where's the horses?"

"Why, they're right outside."

"I want them in here. You bring them in."

Half an hour later Murphy was mounted on a small bay mare. The doctor had done a good job of cleaning and packing the bullet wound in his side, stating that he didn't think it was too serious unless it became infected or started bleeding again.

A lariat was tied solid to Murphy's saddle horn. The other end, the loop end, was tightly fitted around Williams's neck. The man was sitting a fleabitten gray ahead of Murphy, and his face was completely drained of color.

"Williams," Murphy said, "you understand the way this deal is going to work, don't you? Anything goes wrong outside, doesn't matter what or whose fault it is, and you get a load of buckshot in the back.

"You better keep a real tight rein on your horse, too. If he spooks and runs from, say, a gunshot, the rope will break your neck like it was a dry twig. You might want to explain that to those good folks out there."

"I will." Williams's voice was shaky. "I'll do exactly what you tell me."

"All right, Doc," Murphy said. "Open the door. When we get outside there should be a sweat-caked dun at the hitch rail. You untie him and wrap the reins around my saddle horn."

The doctor moved to the door, opening it wide.

"Start your horse," Murphy said to Williams. "Hold him slow."

A few steps brought the gray to the opening. The horse shied sideways away from it, refusing to go through. Murphy held his breath. The last thing he wanted was a wreck. Williams was no good to him dead.

He nudged the bay mare forward a little. The amount of slack in the rope had to be carefully maintained. Too much and the gray could get a hoof over it and become tangled, in which case Williams would be dragged beneath him. Too little and the slightest unexpected movement would jerk the man out of the saddle.

Williams began to coax the gray, speaking to him gently and patting his neck. Finally, in a hurried blur of motion, Williams bent low, the gray stepped through, and Murphy spurred the bay to keep up.

Outside, a concrete porch landing and steps slowed the horses as they picked their way down, the sound of their iron shoes loud on the hard surface. When both horses reached the ground, a few of the men behind the barricades stood up, aiming their rifles. Williams stopped the gray.

"Do not fire. Do you see this rope? Any action by you will insure my death. Put down your weapons."

The old doctor led the dun beside Murphy and wrapped the reins around the saddle horn as he had been told, then hurried off.

Murphy's voice was loud. "Now, I don't intend to kill this man, but if a single one of you follows us, I will. This is my table, my game, you're up against a stacked deck, and I've got nothing to lose.

"Move out, Williams."

People lined the street in confounded silence. Murphy kept his eyes on his hostage and the rope. Both hammers on the shotgun in his hands were cocked, and he had his finger touching the front trigger.

He felt better than he had earlier, the pain in his side wasn't quite as severe, and the queasiness had subsided somewhat. And it looked as if he were going to ride right through town with more reverence than the governor would get at the head of a parade.

Soon Prescott lay behind them. Murphy looked back occasionally, unable to see anyone following. Yet he didn't believe for a second that his threat would hold. A posse was bound to come, staying at a distance.

"Head west a little," he told Williams.

When they reached the draw where Murphy had left Dodson's black, he dismounted and tied the horse to Williams's saddle horn, then tied the dun he had been leading to the saddle horn on the black.

With the two fresh horses he probably wouldn't need the black, yet San Patricio was a long way off and the extra mount, though hard used, might come in handy.

He moved close to Williams, pointing the shotgun at him. "I'm going to let you breathe a little easier. Take the rope off your neck and put it on your horse."

The truth was Murphy could care less about Williams's comfort. The slack in the rope between them required too much attention, and out here in open country it served no purpose except to slow them down.

Williams removed the loop and settled it over the gray's head, then rubbed his throat. A look of genuine appreciation was on his face. "Thank you."

Murphy remounted the mare and rode past him, coiling the slack in the rope as he went and pulling the three-horse train into action. "You sit there and don't make a move unless I tell you to."

Hours later, as the sun was about to set, Murphy glimpsed a large group of riders top a low swell and then disappear a mile or more behind them. This was the fourth time he'd seen the posse, and it appeared that with the coming of nightfall the group was drawing closer.

He continued on, leading the horses in a trot. Williams hadn't spoken since leaving the draw where the black had been tied and neither had Murphy.

At last the night darkness was complete and Murphy stopped. His blood loss had created an unquenchable thirst, and he uncorked his canteen, drinking the last swallow in it.

He was exhausted, feverish, and his side felt like it was on fire. And he had reached a decision. For the most part the posses he had been in were composed of family men who, unless the issue involved them personally, quickly tired of the chase and started looking for a reason, any reason, that would allow them to return home.

Williams, who had earlier been such a vital part of his escape, was now a hindrance to it. As long as Murphy had him, the posse would follow relentlessly. But if he let him go, there was a strong likelihood that most, if not all, of the men in it, would take Williams back to Prescott, rejoicing in their partial victory.

And there was another reason for allowing Williams to go free. Murphy realized his strength was fading like water dripping from a leaky bucket. He'd do his best to sit the saddle night and day until he reached San Patricio, yet what if he couldn't, what if he fell to the ground unconscious. Williams would be there to kill him.

"Climb down," Murphy told Williams. "The trip's over for you."

Williams stepped off the gray. "You aren't going to shoot me, are you? I know I shouldn't have tried to have you arrested. I was frightened by you, terrified. I was afraid of what you might do. It was a mistake. Please, I beg you."

"You know, Williams, I believe you. You really don't know who Ben King is, do you?"

"No. I swear it. I never heard of him."

For a moment Murphy considered taking the time to tell Wiliams the rest of his story, the part about the mine and the slaves, but he decided against it. He had trusted the man once too many times already.

He wiped at a gnat on his ear. "There's a posse behind us a mile or two. Stay here and they'll find you. When they do, tell them what a nice fellow I am for letting you go. Tell them to get off my trail and stay off or I'll take the buffalo gun out of my scabbard and start using it."

Murphy nudged the mare on, leading the three saddled horses. He didn't look back at the well-dressed man standing alone in the darkness. His thoughts were on the miles ahead.

Whether the posse continued to follow him or not, his best shot at reaching San Patricio was to travel as fast as he could. He'd continue to ride the mare until she was spent, then unsaddle her and turn her loose. Then he'd do the same with the gray, and last the black. The dun was his horse, he'd had him a long time, and he'd try to keep him.

CHAPTER 15

THE CRUNCHING OF hooves on sand and gravel stirred Al Murphy. As he turned over, pain from his side ripped through him, half-waking him. The noise stopped, and instinctively Murphy reacted to the subconscious warning that had served him so well for so many years.

His eyes flew open and he reached for the Colt in his holster.

"I wouldn't if'n I was you, Marshal."

Murphy had his hand on the Colt's grip. If it hadn't been for the calm, almost nonchalant flow of the deep voice, he would have pulled it and taken his chances. Instead he turned his head to see a giant of a man standing a few feet from him.

He blinked against the sunlight, then weakly sat up, trying to remember where he had seen the familiar black-bearded face. At last his somnolent mind triggered. He was looking at the miner he had fought in the saloon in Vera Cruz because the man had refused to give up his gun.

The big man kept his handgun on Murphy. "I come across a black horse, saddled and looking like he's done been to Montana and back. By the lay of the tracks I been followin', I reckon he must belong to you."

Murphy racked his brain. It was night and he was riding the black horse while leading the dun. Knowing the black's strength was about gone, he had managed to shift into the saddle on the dun without dismounting. Too feeble to do anything about unsaddling, he had turned the black loose as he was.

Afterward he rode, but not far. The last thing he remembered was doing his best to keep from falling off the dun.

Murphy tried to speak but could only manage a hoarse whisper that could not be understood. The miner let the hammer down on his revolver and shoved it into his waistband.

"Don't look to me like you're able to do much fightin', and if'n you was gonna shoot me you'd a done it that day in Vera Cruz."

He went to his pack mule, which stood behind him beside the black, and lifted the corner of a pannier tarp and pulled out a bottle.

"A little whiskey'll loosen up that throat of yours. Ain't nothin' works better, 'cept maybe a touch of coal oil and I ain't got none of that."

The whiskey did help, enough so that Murphy could speak of what he wanted and needed the most.

"Water."

Most of a canteen later, along with a few more pulls from the bottle, Murphy felt better. He knew it was his loss of blood that made him so thirsty, and if he hadn't gotten the water he could not have lasted long. Whether the big miner who was setting a pot of beans to boil on a mesquite fire knew it or not, he had saved Murphy's life, and considering what had happened between them, that was something.

"Friend," Murphy said, surprised at the volume of his gravelly voice. "Thanks. I owe you and I'm sorry about the trouble we had."

The miner stood. "You whipped me fair and square enough. Ain't nobody else ever done it and darned few that ever had the guts to try. I got no use for a coward and you surely ain't one. You coulda hid behind your badge and shot me down and got clean away with it, but you didn't. You got sand, son. You come at me straight, the hard way."

"You're right about that." Murphy rose slowly to his feet,

testing the strength in his legs. He took a step. "It was hard enough so that I don't want to ever have to try it again."

He held out his hand. "I'm not the marshal of Vera Cruz anymore. Name's Al Murphy, and like I said, I owe you."

Murphy felt his hand become lost in the miner's grip. "Sam Bundy here."

The man knelt to stir the beans and add more wood to the fire. "You know it was a week before I could see after that poundin' you gave me. My ribs are still a little sore from you swingin' that shotgun barrel around."

"I didn't feel too good afterward, either."

Sam grinned. "Guess that brings me some comfort."

The dun snorted, drawing Murphy's attention. The horse had left the sparse bunch grass he had been nibbling on and was joining the black and Bundy's blue roan.

Sam gestured with his thumb at Murphy's blood-crusted shirt. "Looks like you picked you up a little lead somewhere. The slug still in ya?"

"No, it just cut through the side. A doctor patched it up and I don't think it's bled much since."

Sam said no more. If Murphy wanted to tell him about what had happened, that was fine, but it was the custom of western men not to pry into affairs that were not their own.

Murphy stepped back to the canteen he had been drinking from and picked it up. "This all the water you're carrying?"

"Help yourself. They's another canteen full on the mule. We ain't no more'n twelve miles outta San Patricio and that's where I'm headin'. I'll be there tonight."

Twelve miles, Murphy thought. *I almost made it.*

A gnawing hunger filled him as he finished the last of the water in the canteen. He eyed the saddlebags on the dun. "I've got some jerky that would go good with those beans."

"Bring it on. The more the better. We'll have us a little feast."

After they had finished eating, Murphy changed into

the new shirt Risa had sent with him, unsaddled the dun, brushed him with a metal pocket comb, and put the saddle back on. The food, water, and hours of rest had revived him, and other than an acute stiffness in his side that made his movements awkward, he felt better than could be expected.

A sense of urgency flooded through him. Three hours of daylight remained, and the quicker he reached San Patricio the better.

He mounted the dun, holding the black's reins in his right hand. He would just as soon have unsaddled the black and turned him loose, but Sam wouldn't understand the action and he didn't want to tell the man he was a horse thief. Besides, this trail wasn't over, wouldn't be over at San Patricio, and once again the horse might prove useful.

Bundy was tightening the lash ropes over the pack on the mule. Murphy nudged the roan closer to him. "Sam, I'm obliged to you. I'm going to San Patricio myself, and we could go in together except there's something you have to know. The law's after me. A posse could show up at any time and I'd rather not get you mixed up in my troubles."

Acting as if he hadn't heard Murphy, Sam continued his work until he was finished, then took hold of the mule's lead rope.

"I guess you think nobody knows nothin' about you. Nobody knows about Marshal Dodson takin' you out of Vera Cruz, wearin' handcuffs in broad daylight. Ain't nobody knows that Ben King's the one that had it done 'cause you braced him in front of his men about wearin' guns in town. Shoot, that monkey court that was gonna hang you in Tucson and you shootin' them deputies up there is the talk of half the territory.

"Ain't nobody done nothin' though, and they ain't goin' to. They're all afraid of King and Dodson and they keep as clear from trouble with 'em as they can. I ain't no different, long as I'm left alone to do my drinkin' and pros-pectin' whenever and wherever I please. But two days ago King done made hisself a big mistake. My partner and me was workin' a little color about fifteen miles north of his big silver mine and—"

"You mean you know about the mine?" Murphy interrupted excitedly. "You know about the Apache slaves working there?"

"Course I do. There's others know about it too. Cain't keep somethin' as big as that a secret. He bought them Indians from a bunch of army revolutionaries down in Mexico, least that's what I heard. King's a rich man in this country, already owns most of it, and he's got hisself a small army of hired killers. Ever'body stays as clear of him as they can and there ain't no law to go to about it anyhow. He owns 'em all, judges included. Why, I wouldn't be a bit surprised if the governor wasn't on the payroll, too."

"I'm afraid you may be right about that. I went to his office in Prescott and barely made it out of there alive."

"Well, as I was sayin', my partner and me was workin' a little color, mindin' our own business. I went into Vera Cruz for some whiskey and things. When I got back, Jeb was layin' there dead. Four bullet holes in him."

"How do you know it was King who did it?"

"Tracked their horses to within shoutin' distance of his mine. Whether King was with 'em or not, it's the same difference. They was his men and he's responsible. After that I was circlin' around to get to San Patricio when I come across you. I ain't goin' into town for no grub. I need me a long gun, maybe one of them Henry repeaters. My old single-shot Springfield ain't up to the task.

"And"—Sam's eyes narrowed—"I aim to get hold of a box of dynamite. King's done made hisself a big mistake, and I'm here to dang sure see that he pays for it."

Sam mounted his horse and, leading the mule, took off in a trot. Murphy spurred the dun. He started to tell Sam that he didn't stand a chance against King's army, that there had to be a better way, then caught himself. For too long that had been the bent of his thinking and what had it changed? King was still in the driver's seat, running roughshod over everyone and everything.

Murphy mentally kicked himself. If Santiago, Froylan, and Antonio were at the mine, had he waited too long? Would they still be alive?

A terrific surge of anger welled up in Murphy, most of it directed at King, but part of it aimed at himself. Risa had written him asking for help and the only thing he had done was traipse all over the country doing his best to get himself killed and accomplishing nothing.

Starting now, Murphy resolved, that was going to change. He had tried to use the law and the authorities to avoid a lot of needless bloodshed and had run into a block wall at every turn. Because of his visit to Prescott and the rough treatment he had given Gene Williams, every lawman in the territory would be doubling their efforts to bring him in.

No, regardless of the odds, there was but one thing left to do. And it must be done very quickly.

CHAPTER 16

GABRIEL RACED OUT of the Villabisencio house and through the garden in the fading, evening sunlight. "Señor Murphy."

When the boy reached him, Murphy's reception was natural, automatic. He picked him up, wincing slightly from his sore side, and held him close. "It's good to see you, Gabriel. I've missed you."

Risa was coming out of the house, and Murphy set the boy down.

"It is a good thing you were not here," Gabriel said excitedly. "Marshal Dodson and a bunch of men, they came and went to every house in the village looking for you. They came here, but I hid from them in the field. I am very good at hiding you know. They did not see me."

Risa stepped up and Murphy turned to the large man standing near him. "Sam, this is Risa Villabisencio."

Sam removed his hat. "Pleasure to meet you, ma'am."

"And this," Murphy said, ruffling Gabriel's hair, "is Gabriel."

Murphy looked at Risa. "I hear you had a visit from Dodson and a posse. Did they give you much trouble?"

"No. Fortunately el señor Pena sent a man here to warn us that they were coming. Gabriel hid out in the field. When they came, the marshal's men searched everywhere, but he did not get down from his horse."

She pulled a loose strand of hair from her face. "Did you see the governor? Is he going to help us?"

It was hard for Murphy to continue to look into her trusting eyes. "I'm sorry, Risa. I shouldn't have wasted the

119

time to go to Prescott. We'll put the horses up, and then I'll tell you about it."

Risa's chin dropped, and he could tell her disappointment was almost more than she could bear. He placed his hand on her shoulder.

"We're going to the mine tonight. Win or lose, we'll do everything we possibly can. Sam has his own reasons for hating Ben King, and he thinks the man stays out at his mine most of the time. He and I have talked some. He knows about Santiago and the boys and we've got a plan, at least part of one. Do you think you could get Pena to come over and talk with us?"

Her face brightened. "He will come. Gabriel can go to the store and bring him here while I prepare you something to eat."

After caring for the horses, Murphy and Sam went into the kitchen, washed, and sat down at the table to the cups of steaming coffee Risa had set there. While she worked at the stove, Murphy told her about what he had seen at the mine, everything that had happened in Prescott, including the wound he had received and his narrow escape, and finally his meeting with Sam. She listened with only an occasional nod and had just finished placing a pot of chicken stew, a stack of tortillas, and five bowls on the table when Gabriel and Pena came into the room.

Murphy rose from his chair. He hadn't seen Pena since the first time he'd come to San Patricio when he had stayed with the Villabisencios to recover from the head wound he had received in the cantina gun fight.

The man looked old, his long beard completely white, yet his black eyes were clear, quick, and direct. His tan pants and white shirt were spotless and neatly pressed.

"It's good to see you again," Murphy shook hands. "You look to be in good health."

"Thank you, señor Murphy. You also appear to be well."

Murphy was glad he had changed out of his bloody shirt.

There was so much dirt, sweat, and saddle grime on his pants that the man didn't notice the blood stains on them. He turned to Sam and made the introduction. When the men were seated, Risa poured more coffee and everyone helped themselves to the stew.

"Señor Pena," Murphy said, after eating a bite. "I'm sure Risa has told you I went to see the governor. It's a long story and I've already told it once, but there will be no help from that end. I've tried everything I can think of with no luck, and I probably don't have much time left in Arizona. I'm an escaped convict, wanted for murder, and sooner or later a posse or bounty hunter is sure to get me. If Santiago is at the mine and I'm going to do anything to help him, I have to do it now, tonight."

He continued. "Before I left for Prescott, Risa said you were gathering men and weapons to go to the mine and fight. I'd like to hear what you had in mind."

Pena shrugged. "I was only beginning to do whatever I could. Santiago has been my friend and the friend of many others in the valley for many years. When Risa told me you were going to see the governor and that my actions would perhaps cause many deaths that Santiago would not approve of, I stopped. Because I had not yet sent scouts to the mine to determine the terrain and the force of the opposition, I had no detailed plan for the attack."

Murphy was surprised at Pena's use of military language and it was a moment before he remembered that the man had been an officer in the Mexican War.

He took a sip of coffee. "I've been to the mine, and so has Sam here. It's at one end of a deep, box canyon which, as best as we know, has just one way in or out of it. There are at least thirty men guarding the place. We've talked some, and we don't think any kind of a direct attack will work, even if we had the men it would take to make it. The attack could also put the workers in the middle of cross fire where a good number of them are liable to be shot.

"What we need"—Murphy scratched his ear—"is a diversion. Something big enough to cause the guards to leave the canyon to investigate."

"An explosion's what he's a-gettin' at," Sam interjected. "We need a load of dynamite or a little nitro to set off a-ways from the entrance to the canyon so them guards'll hightail it outta there to have themselves a look see. When they do, and they're up purt near to the top, we'll hit 'em with more dynamite and all the lead we can rain down on 'em."

A smile spread across Pena's face. "Now I know why President Antonio Santa Anna could not win the war against you. You plan well. Sometimes I sell dynamite to the miners in the area. There are several boxes of it and two rolls of fuse in the shed behind the store."

"Good," Murphy said. "That should do. I know I was the one who stopped you from gathering the men and I still don't like the idea one bit, but we've got no choice. How many do you think you can come up with who have guns and know how to use them?"

"There are more than you might think. Of course, the men here are poor farmers but most of them, especially the older ones, have had to fight Apache raiders many times to protect their families and their homes.

"There are as many as twenty men in the valley who have guns and can use them well. Before I stopped what I was doing, I managed to gather nine lever-action repeating rifles. Three of them are my own."

Murphy's thoughts went to the road he had seen leading up the gorge and out of the canyon. If he and Sam could get rid of the guards that were stationed there before dawn and position the farmers behind boulders, they should be fairly safe. Everything would have to be carefully timed so that when daylight came and the explosion took place, no one started shooting until most of the men guarding the mine were in the gorge, making their way to the top.

"Well," Murphy said. "We'd better get busy. Sam and I will work on details. We'll make a map showing where everything is and where everyone needs to be. Mister Pena, you'll need to get the men, guns, ammunition, and dynamite here just as quick as you can. Before we leave for the mine, everybody has to have a clear understanding of what we are going to do."

Risa folded her arms. "What if you do this? What if you risk your lives and some of you are killed and my husband and sons are not at the mine?"

"Won't bother me none," Sam said, leaning back in his chair. " 'Cept I a-course hope they're there. King's got some trouble due that's comin' at him from me one way or the other. This is just a whole lot bigger and better than I could do by myself."

"Same with me," Murphy said quietly. "At least this way we'll know, and regardless, the slaves at the mine need to be set free."

"And Risa"—Pena stroked his beard—"have you forgotten the two herders from our village who were murdered by Ben King? Those men had families. If King is not stopped he will eventually come into the valley to take the land, and more of us will die."

"Yes, yes. You are right. It is only that what you had told me, Al, is true. Santiago is a gentle man. He hates violence. He would not want anyone to be hurt because of him."

"There's no other way I know of except to forget it, and we can't do that," Murphy said, reaching in his shirt pocket for his tobacco sack. "I've got to get out of Arizona, and if I'm going to be any help at all, it has to be now."

Mister Pena stood. "I had better be leaving. There is a great deal to do."

Gabriel had been listening intently to everything that had been said while busily shoveling in stew, tortillas, and honey. "Wait, señor Pena. I will go with you. There is something at your store I will need to buy for the trip."

"You're not going with us to the mine, Gabriel," Murphy said sternly. "You're staying here with Risa."

"I think I will go there. You might need me to do something. It is a very good thing that I have helped you before. I think maybe I will not charge you any money."

"Doesn't matter what you think. You're not going, and if I have to tie you up to keep you here, I will."

CHAPTER 17

MURPHY CREPT IN the darkness toward the spot where he had earlier seen the faint glow of a cigarette. Nervous energy filled him; his legs felt like tightly coiled springs. Each step he took was carefully tested. The slightest noise would warn the guard of his approach and destroy everything they were trying to do.

He reached a large rock and inched around it, hardly breathing. He knew he must be close, yet when he saw the silhouette of the guard standing no more than four feet away it shocked him, and it was all he could do to keep from rushing the man.

One more step. Murphy raised the knife in his hand. The guard wheeled as if warned by a premonition, and Murphy lunged at him, locking his left arm around the man's throat and sticking the knife blade deep into his chest. The guard went limp, and Murphy released his hold, letting him drop to the ground.

Murphy stepped back against the rock to catch his breath. A sickening feeling was in his guts, the same feeling he'd had after killing the two cowboys in Vera Cruz. Why? he wondered. Why was it that everything he became involved with ended up in violence and death? Surely other people didn't live this way.

He forced himself to quit thinking about it, instead focusing his thoughts on Sam. The big miner was somewhere on the other side of the gorge trying to do the same thing he had just done—provided a guard was stationed there. It was unlikely that more than two men had been posted to guard the road entrance at this late hour, yet he and Sam had to cover the ground to make certain.

Murphy went to the dead man and pulled him around behind the rock, hiding him so that when daylight came, the body could not be seen. He took the man's revolver, Winchester rifle, and cartridge belt, then continued to walk slowly and carefully while searching with his eyes and ears for the telltale sign of another sentry.

After having walked the rough, narrow wagon road a fourth of the way down into the canyon and back up again, Murphy approached a barren spot of flat on top where he and Sam had agreed to meet. The big man was standing there, outlined against the starry sky and looking somewhat like one of the giant saguaro cactuses scattered around Tuscon.

"It's me, Sam," Murphy whispered. He stepped up close. "I found one. How'd you come out?"

"One. Broke his neck and got his long gun. He's all I could find."

"Well, guess we've done everything we can. There's other guards scattered along the canyon rim, but they're far enough away they shouldn't bother us as long as we don't make too much noise."

Sam looked at the sky. "Ain't got more'n an hour or so 'fore dawn. Reckon Pena ought to be done gettin' the dynamite set for the startin' blowout a-this here party. I'll start runnin' fuse and gettin' the charges set and ready along the road in the gorge."

Murphy nodded in the darkness. "I'll get the men and position them where they need to be. When I'm through, I'll meet you in the road about halfway down the canyon."

Murphy crouched behind an egg-shaped boulder about the right height to rest his rifle over when standing. The lever-action Winchester and the pistol he had taken from the guard were fully loaded, along with the Colt he had and the Remington buffalo gun he'd gotten from the blacksmith. In all, he could fire twenty-nine shots without stopping to reload.

The gray of dawn was closing in. It wouldn't be long. Pena was supposed to start setting off the series of dynamite charges as soon as it was light enough to see. Fourteen men from the village had rifles and were well hidden in the gorge on both sides of the road. Five others were with Pena to take care of the rim guards when they came running and to stop any of the guards in the gorge from breaking through at the top.

Sam and Murphy were positioned across the road from each other at the low end of the trap. Any of the guards who tried to get back down into the canyon were going to have to go through them.

Murphy wiped his red, swollen eyes with his fingers. He was physically and mentally exhausted and the only thing keeping him going was a stubborn, determined will mixed with anxiety and apprehension over what he and the others were attempting to do.

His thoughts went to Risa. If the strike was successful and it turned out that Santiago and her sons weren't at the mine, the news would devastate her. He would have no choice but to stay in Arizona and continue to try to help her, but with so many in the territory hunting him, how could he?

Unable to think of an answer, Murphy shrugged the question off. Life came one trail at a time, and he hadn't finished riding the one he was on.

He looked below. Already he could see the vague figures of men scurrying about on the canyon floor. Pena could not afford to wait much longer. The day guards would be going to relieve the night shift.

Minutes dragged by. Murphy looked up the road and

gorge, glad that he was unable to see any of the men he had placed there. He looked across the road. Sam was hidden from sight.

Although he was expecting it, the explosion surprised him. He was amazed at the deafening roar, the vibrating ground, and the huge cloud of smoke and dust that billowed into the sky.

He looked down into the canyon and saw a frantic blur of activity. Several men with rifles emerged from the rest. The plan was working. They were coming.

Pena's second charge of dynamite went off, sounding and feeling much like the first. Rather than one explosion to create the diversion, they had decided on three so that a sense of urgency would be maintained among the guards. Six minutes from now Pena would set off the final charge.

Murphy continued to hide behind the rock. The road leading out of the canyon was fast filling with armed men from the mine, and more were coming, some of them mounted on horses.

Timing was everything. No one was supposed to fire a shot until the front mine guards were almost to the top. When that first shot came, Sam would light the fuse to the dynamite charges he had placed in the road and every man would start shooting.

The mounted riders Murphy had seen were getting closer. He could hear the rapid hoofbeats of their horses. He wanted to rise up and take a look, but he forced himself not to. If he or a single man above were seen, it would seriously jeopardize the operation.

Pena's third dynamite charge blew. Shortly thereafter a lone rifle shot boomed, followed by an unrelenting storm of thunderous shots. Murphy stood, rested the Winchester on the rock, and started firing at a couple of men who were less than a hundred yards below him. They fell, and he shifted his aim to the line of running, bewildered men above.

The first of Sam's dynamite charges blew, followed by another and another. Dust, smoke, and rock fragments boiled into the air. Men were yelling, screaming, and the solid roar of gunshots thickened.

Murphy fired at everything that moved in the dense haze until the Winchester clicked empty. He then put a revolver in each hand and rested his elbows on the rock to steady his aim. A running horse and rider appeared, heading back down. Murphy was about to pull the trigger when the rider fell. He knew Sam had to be the one who had fired the fatal shot.

A tight group of four men came running from above. Murphy fired on them until both his revolvers were empty. Not a man was left standing. He picked up the Remington buffalo gun, noticing that the rumble of gunshots was fast waning.

Two riders rushed down the gorge at a dead run. In the thick dust it was hard to be sure, but the one closest to him was riding a buckskin that looked an awful lot like Marshal Dodson's.

There was no time to think, no time to take careful aim. Murphy pulled the hammer back on the rifle, threw it to his shoulder, and pulled the trigger. The gun bucked in his hands and pounded his shoulder. The rider plunged to the ground.

A series of quick shots came from Sam's position, and the other rider slid from his horse. Less than a minute later all shooting had ceased. A wave of bluish-black smoke hung in the air, and the stench of burnt gunpowder was strong.

Murphy finished reloading the Winchester and one of the revolvers. He stepped out from the rock. "You all right, Sam?"

"Yep," the big miner stood and started walking toward Murphy while thumbing shells into the magazine of his rifle. "Ain't none of 'em even got a shot off at me. Never seen nothin' work no better. They likely ain't a durned one of them sorry varmints left."

Murphy stepped to the sprawled body of the man he had shot off the buckskin horse. Dodson's lifeless gray eyes stared up at him.

Sam moved alongside him. "He was hooked up with King tighter than a knot in a wet rope. Reckon that's one crooked law dog that won't be botherin' you or nobody else no more."

The quiet after so much noise bothered Murphy. "We better get on down there, Sam. You take the left side and I'll take the right. Keep your eyes open. There could be a few of them left."

They found the bed of the canyon still. Nothing moved. Since the slave miners wouldn't have a clue what the commotion was about, the only thing Murphy could figure was that they had all gone into the mine for protection.

Murphy walked toward the large, piecemeal building he had sighted from the canyon rim the day he had started for Prescott. He was almost to the open door when a voice called from behind.

"Señor Murphy."

He wheeled and as he did, the report of a gunshot ripped through the queer calm. A bullet whined past his ear and he dropped to the ground spinning, trying to determine where the shot had come from.

"Get down, Gabriel," he yelled. Another shot came, the bullet striking the earth inches from his face. Murphy saw the glint of a rifle barrel poking out the window of the solid, railroad-timbered structure some sixty yards away. He rolled to the side, levering a round into the Winchester as he went, and came up shooting with the rifle against his shoulder.

Glass broke in the window, and the barrel that had been there disappeared. Murphy ran to the building, flattening himself against a corner. He glanced back to where he had seen Gabriel. The boy was gone, but he saw Sam crouched low and running toward him from the other side of the canyon.

He stepped around the corner, leaped across the opening of another window, and stopped a few feet from the door.

"Listen in there," Murphy propped the rifle against the wall and pulled the Colt. "Twenty men will be here in a few minutes. You haven't got a chance. Come out with your hands up and empty."

"That you, Al Murphy?"

The voice sounded faintly familiar, but Murphy couldn't place it. "Who am I talking to?"

"It's Ben King. Look, I know we've had our differences, but we can still put all that behind us. I can give you a life like you've never dreamed of. You want a ranch and six thousand head of cattle, you've got it. I'll throw in a saloon, a freight company. Let me ride out of here and it's yours. You'll never have to work another day in your life."

"Your offer interests me," Murphy lied. "Step out here and we'll talk about it. If you don't I'll burn you out and then I'll do the same thing you tried to do to me. I'll hang you."

It was a long moment before King spoke. "I'm going to the door. Hold your fire."

The door creaked open. King had one foot out. Murphy's grip on the Colt tightened.

A shot boomed, echoing loudly against the canyon walls, and King stumbled headlong into the dirt, a six-gun in his hand.

Sam ambled up, the muzzle of his rifle smoking. "Sure am glad to see ole man King didn't miss this here party. I wanted him more'n anybody." He kicked the body over with the toe of his boot. "I done killed him too quick though. Bullet went plumb through his heart."

A moan came from inside. Murphy held the Colt ready and warily stepped through the door. A man was sitting on the floor beneath the window he had shot through earlier. Harry Walcott was clutching his bloody middle with both hands.

"I might have known you were on King's payroll." Murphy moved close to him. "Why did you hire me as marshal? How much did he pay you to keep from showing up at my trial in Tucson?"

Walcott didn't speak, and in a sudden rage Murphy grabbed his hair and yanked his head back.

"Answer me!"

"I . . . I hired you because Vera Cruz needed you. It was later . . . later that King threatened to kill me and the others in town if we tried to help you. He—"

Murphy slapped him with the back of his hand. "How much? You wouldn't be here if you weren't working for King."

Walcott groaned. His eyes bugged out wide and he jerked upward in agony, then fell to the floor and lay still. Murphy stared at him in disgust, then turned to see Sam standing in the doorway.

"Friend a-yours, uh?"

"Yeah."

They stepped outside. Pena was riding toward them on his sorrel and leading Murphy's dun. Beside him, Risa was riding Dodson's black. Farther behind, the men from the village were walking in a single file, holding their rifles against their shoulders.

Gabriel came running from wherever he had been hiding. "Señor Murphy. It is a very good thing I have come to here. That man at the window might have killed you if I had not called to you."

"Won't work, Gabriel," Murphy scolded. "I told you to stay at Risa's. What are you doing here?"

"I did stay there, but then I think you might need my help like you did in Tucson and I followed the tracks to here. I am very good at following tracks, you know, and also at making them to disappear."

Murphy tried to act angry but couldn't. Risa stepped off the black and ran over to Gabriel, hugging him. "Thank God you are all right." She glanced at Murphy. "When I found out he had left I knew where he had gone and I had to come."

Pena nudged his horse closer, regarding King's body with disdain. He shifted his gaze to Murphy. "Where are the slaves?"

"Hiding in the mine, I guess. That's the only place they can be. How many men did we lose?"

A broad smile spread across Pena's smudged face. "Every man is here."

Murphy collected his rifle and shoved it in the dun's scabbard.

"Look!" Gabriel yelled, pointing to the end of the canyon where the mine entrance was.

A throng of men came pouring toward them. Risa hurried toward the slaves. Two men, shirtless and wearing leg chains, broke from the rest and hobbled as fast as they could to meet her.

"Froylan! Antonio!" she cried.

The sight of the three holding each other made Murphy believe that everything he had been through had been worthwhile. When the crowd of slaves drew closer, he studied them. They were filthy, half-starved, barely alive, and it looked as if there were nearly as many Mexicans among them as there were Apaches.

"Sure a pitiful lookin' bunch, ain't it?" Sam spoke as much to himself as anyone else.

Murphy glanced up at Pena. "Looks like Santiago didn't make it."

The man nodded solemnly, then kicked his horse and rode to where Risa and her sons were standing. Murphy handed the dun's reins to Gabriel and walked out to face the slaves who were apprehensively watching the line of armed men from the village.

"All of you," Murphy said as loudly as he could. "You are free to go. Take any of the food that is here. Take whatever you want from here and leave."

Many of them shouted and most started running. As he watched the group scatter like a huge covey of frightened quail, a restlessness grew in Murphy. He too wanted to leave, to get on the dun and ride. It wasn't just that it was still risky for him to be in Arizona. He didn't belong in this canyon, didn't belong in this territory. The county jail at Turrett, New Mexico, was his home, or as close to a home as anything he'd had in years.

He turned around and gazed at Gabriel, who was stroking the dun's nose. The boy was about the only thing here he was really going to miss.

Pena, Risa, and her sons crowded around him. The young men didn't look anything like the small boys he remembered, but he could still see a hint of their mother in their faces.

"Froylan?" Murphy offered his hand to the taller of the two.

"Yes, señor Murphy. It is me." Froylan disregarded the hand and hugged Murphy, as did Antonio. Both men as well as their mother had tears streaming down their cheeks.

"Santiago is gone," Risa said, her chin lifting. "The blood on the buggy seat was his. His body is buried inside the mine."

Murphy stared at the ground. "I'm sorry."

She took his hand in hers. "Do not be sad. Thank you

for all that you have done. God has given me back my sons, and in them a part of Santiago will never die. He will be with us forever."

In a moment Murphy raised his head. "Guess I need to be getting on back to New Mexico. Will you—"

"You are not leaving now, are you?" Risa interrupted. "You must stay with us a few days until you are rested."

"No, I appreciate it, but I have to be going. There's a long trail ahead of me. I need to ask a favor of you though. Would you look after Gabriel for me? He doesn't have anyone else."

"Of course I will, Al, but you must know that it will break his heart for you to leave. He thinks of you as his father, he looks up to you as a hero. You are his best friend and he trusts you. When you were gone to Prescott he would speak of no one else."

Murphy removed his hat and ran his fingers through his thinning hair. "I can't take him with me. I don't even have a house. A jail is no place to raise a boy, and I'm gone from it most of the time. Gabriel needs a woman, a mother. He needs to go to school and make something of himself like Santiago did."

"There are no schools in New Mexico?" Pena asked, an amused twinkle in his eye. "There is not a woman there who would be willing to help you with the boy?"

Risa touched Murphy's arm. "I will try to do anything you ask of me, but Gabriel has a mind of his own. You are the only one he respects. I do not think he will stay in San Patricio. He will either try to follow you or he will go back to Vera Cruz."

Murphy shrugged, putting his hat on. Maybe Risa and Pena were right. He did know a woman in Turrett who he was sure would help, and there was a small school there. A light feeling came over him as if a heavy yoke had been lifted from his shoulders.

He smiled. "Thanks, both of you. I didn't want to have

to tell him goodbye. Didn't know how I was going to be able to."

Pena shook Murphy's hand. "I will miss you, señor. None of this"—he gestured at the canyon walls—"would have been possible without you."

Murphy remembered Oberling's letter and reached in his pocket and handed it to Pena. "Don't know if that will help much, but it might. Since my trail's too hot for me to stick around, I'm counting on all of you to try and clear my name."

He looked at Risa. "You know when I was in Prescott I never did see the governor. He might help if he knew about everything. Maybe you could write him a letter. Be sure and mention Thomas Oberling and Judge Perkins in Tucson and what they tried to do to me.

"I'm afraid the law here is going to have a hard time of it if they try to extradite me back into the territory, but if you need me to testify to anything, send a note."

Froylan spoke. "My father spent his life fighting for justice for everyone. I will follow in his footsteps. I will go to Prescott and see the governor. If it is necessary, I will go to see the president in Washington."

"Thanks, son," Murphy said. "Santiago was a great man. I know if he were here he'd be proud of you."

Murphy turned and walked to the giant who was still standing near Gabriel. "Sam, I'm pullin' out. If you're ever up New Mexico way, stop by Turrett and I'll buy you all you can drink so long as you promise not to do any fighting."

Sam grinned, and Murphy felt his hand once again become lost in the miner's powerful grip. "I done learned my lesson. You be watchin'. I'm liable to show up there quicker than you think."

Murphy took the reins from Gabriel and mounted the dun. The boy put his hands in his pockets and backed slowly away from the horse.

"Well," Murphy said. "You coming?"

Gabriel looked up, his face beaming. "Me? You want for me to come with you?"

"If that's what you want to do."

Sam grabbed the boy under the arms and swung him on behind. Murphy waved goodbye and spurred the dun into a trot.

Gabriel wrapped his arms around Murphy's waist. "You might have a job for me to do in New Mexico that will pay me a lot of money?"

"Doubt it. You're going to school."

"I do not want to go to school."

"Doesn't matter. You're going anyway."

"I do not think I will go."

"You're going and that's the end of it."

A few minutes later Gabriel spoke again. "You are *leaving,* aren't you?"

"Yeah, that's what we're doing. We're leaving."

"You told me when you were leaving you would give me your badge and the binoculars."

"You bought the only pair of binoculars I have, Gabriel. Remember, I lost mine."

"I know, but you said you would give them to me when you left."

"They're in the saddlebags, Gabriel. The badge too. Help yourself."